VILLA VANESSA

Gary Brun

Cover Illustration and Design
Copyright © 2020 by Kopper Finch
Interior Design by Nina Gibbes
Edited by Kristy Coulcher
Story Edit by Caitlin Hodgson
Thank you to Andrew Lindqvist, James Hoare,
Remy Hii and Joshua Tagg

First Printing, 2020
ISBN: 978-0-6486527-2-4
www.garybrunwrites.com / IG: garybrunwrites

Also by this author,
Coco Was Paradise

For my grandfather.

1

On the quiet avenue, with the shuttered-up gift stores and the half empty cafes, with the bookshops closed for the season and the tourist centre only open on Fridays, the avenue which shimmered with pinks and yellows as the timid, late winter sun cast a dappled haze over the cobbled Mediterranean coast, Paul Greene reached for his camera and took a photo.

It wasn't his first photo in France, he'd photographed France many times before. He'd completed assignments with boyish young models in upmarket Parisian hotels, who'd leave him love letters on cocktail napkins, and football stars so rich they'd order him a Rolex just to say thanks. He'd sat with presidents, with philosophers, and with every-day people too. And then, on some assignments, the ones he enjoyed the most, he'd been alone with nature. Like the time he camped out for weeks as he photographed wild flamingos for National Geographic, snapping away while they taught their young to fish in the murky lagoons of the Camargue.

But this was his first photo on this trip. Paul had been in France now for just over 50 hours, arriving two days previously at six in the morning. He'd flown into Paris and had taken the train from Charles de Gaulle to Gare du Nord, and then the metro from Gare du Nord to Chateau Rouge. From Chateau Rouge he walked the short distance uphill to his hotel in Montmartre.

The morning had been bitterly cold, and when he'd arrived at his hotel, exhausted, he'd been frustrated to learn that he wasn't able to check-in to his room until after 2pm. The hotel was tall and thin, appearing like a tattered book on a shelf, rising out of a tiny block of land barely a few metres wide. Consequently it had no foyer to waste away the hours until he could enter his room, and so he took with him a scarf and some gloves and arranged for his luggage to be stored behind the reception desk where it barely fit. Then he ventured out into the street, which reflected sombre yellow lights under a gentle dusting of early-morning rain. He'd forgotten to travel with an umbrella.

He walked uphill from the hotel until he was in the old artist's district of Montmartre, which had been preserved like a faded photograph tucked away in a cherished album. Occasional murals of Picasso, Toulouse Lautrec and others, painted high on terraced walls of restaurant exteriors, were the only evidence that time had indeed moved on. Any sense of authenticity was nothing more than a cynical illusion, Paul thought, and yet he still found it charming. It was early, not yet eight, with the rare glimpse of sun barely warming the pavement, and the streets, still like the last days of autumn, were almost completely void of life. As the rain fell harder, Paul hurried through the labyrinth of gift stores and cafes and up the stairs to the Sacré Cœur, relieved to find it was already open and willing to accept him.

Inside he admired the mosaic, the largest in France a guide had told him on a trip many years earlier, bursting brilliantly from the heavens with sunburnt golds and electric blues. He marvelled at the stained glass windows, the arches, the piped organ and the toll of the bell. When the rain eased a little he went to the top of the dome and took in the view of the city, as grey as he'd ever seen it. The city was sad, dejected, hidden under cloud. Still reeling from its horror eight or nine months earlier. Still coming to terms with its greatest massacre since the days of revolution. A massacre which had taken Paul's only child, Vanessa. He wanted to cry for her, but he couldn't, he never could. He hadn't cried for her since he'd first heard the news. So instead he said the kind of prayer a non-religious man says, and then he left to find himself a coffee. He'd come to France to find her, but already, just a few hours in, he needed to forget her. He felt sick.

He made his way down the stairs through Le Square Louise Michel, and went along Rue de Steinkerque before turning right at Boulevard de Rochechouart. He continued along Boulevard de Clichy, past the Moulin Rouge and down Rue Blanche. Eventually he found a cafe which suited him, a cafe which was dimly lit and mostly empty. It was heated just enough to take the chill out of his heart and he ordered a plain croissant and a coffee with milk.

Sitting in the warmth of the cafe, Paul began to feel overwhelmed with exhaustion, and almost fell asleep before his coffee had arrived. His flight from Sydney to Dubai had been fine, he'd been placed in an exit row and could stretch out his legs. He'd even managed a few precious hours of sleep. But from Dubai to Paris the plane had been packed to capacity and he was squeezed between two overweight Middle-Eastern men, who seemingly didn't know one another but proceeded to have a conversation for the duration of the flight anyway. When he explained to the hostess that he was too tall to be jammed up like that for eight hours straight, she suggested he have a drink and do his best to relax. So he did drink, but he didn't relax, and as the plane hit turbulence one of the men woke up in a shock and knocked Paul's glass of wine into his lap. He spent the rest of the flight standing by the bathroom, drying his crotch and making apologetic smiles at the line of other passengers waiting to use the toilet.

When he finished the coffee he ordered another, and after two hours in the cafe, reading the newspaper and brushing up on his French, which he was pleased to find was still quite good, he paid his bill and walked down to the Seine. It was past midday now, and the rain had stopped as the clouds broke apart and the city embraced the sunlight. He walked along the Left Bank to Shakespeare and Company, one of his favourite places in the whole city, and smiled at the clerk behind the desk as she welcomed him. As he browsed the shelves he found himself too distracted to be in a bookshop, and so he left. But before leaving he'd purchased a pocket sized journal and a felt-tip pen.

With the Cathedral de Notre Dame in view, Paul sat down to write.

To be in Paris, the city she loved, the city she romanticised since her first visit as a child, to be without her, to be avoiding entire neighbourhoods as the pain is too real, too raw still, 8 months later, as if it were only yesterday, this morning, right now, is some kind of hell.

I have to face it—Paris has changed for me. Forever. And I know for sure I cannot remain. I'll stay tonight, to rest, to drink, to say farewell to the places I've loved.

Tomorrow, if I can, I'll visit the site, then I'll leave on an overnight train for another part of France, a friendlier place from a happier time, and I'll never return.

Paris is dead.

When Paul returned to the hotel, emotionally and physically exhausted, he opened the shutters to his room and let the afternoon breeze sail through. He undressed himself in the fading afternoon light and collapsed like a rag-doll on the tattered mattress. He slept perfectly still until just after nine, when he awoke in a sweat from a nightmare. He'd dreamt of Vanessa, he always did, and it filled him with an unshakeable melancholy. He laid there in the dark, eyes closed tight, trying to forget the dream, while outside on the street he could hear some lively jazz. He remained still for another half hour, willing the music to carry him away to somewhere sweeter, somewhere other than the thought of his daughter's death. Eventually he got up and peered out the window where he could see a small bar opposite the hotel. Despite the threat of rain it was full of people, shuffling in and spilling out on to the street. He got dressed and brushed his teeth, combed his hair and descended the five flights of stairs to street level and went into the bar.

He found an empty stool by the band and ordered a whisky and a beer. The performers were all young, in their early twenties, and he imagined how Vanessa would have enjoyed a night like this, how the music would have brought a smile to her face. Her friends would have been talented, artistic, bohemian, he assumed. He looked around the room at the beautiful young Parisians, barely lit by candlelight, and he realised he was the oldest in the bar by far. If he felt self-conscious, though, it didn't last, as he caught the eye of a mysterious looking blonde in the corner, her glare melting into his own. It made him wonder, what had Vanessa's lovers been like? Were they like the boys in the band, rugged and charismatic, cigarettes dangling from their lips and tattoos up their necks? Were they like the bartender, tall, smartly dressed and muscular, with a thin moustache and slicked-back hair. Or were they like Paul himself? Old and tired and lost, yet somehow handsome? Somehow the most handsome of them all.

As the music continued he allowed the drinks to flow, and as the drinks flowed he descended into a melancholic bliss which felt peaceful and true. He was almost happy, almost ok with the world. The music had such an effect that Paul began to think of her death as something romantic, something noble, like a tragic hero in a Greek fable. If any good had come of her dying, it was that Paul had left his wife, had stopped working so hard, had sold his house, had moved to the other side of the world, had stopped caring about his stocks and his investments and his career. He had no idea how much money he had, he'd lost more than half in the divorce, but his accountant had assured him it'd be enough to last him to his grave, if not further. He felt free, freer than he'd felt since his glory days, his mid-thirties, and even though his heart was heavy without her, it was in another way lighter too. He had managed, since her passing, to find moments to breathe. Paul wasn't religious, far from it, but he'd chosen to believe that her soul was always present, present right now even, as he ordered another drink.

The following day Paul mostly just slept. He didn't bother getting out of bed until the afternoon, when his hangover had faded away and his hunger became too much to ignore. He ate in a small Asian diner a few hundred metres from his hotel, which was brightly lit by flickering bulbs and smelt of raw onion. Outside the diner the streets were gloomy and lifeless, and he made the decision at last that no, he wouldn't visit the place where she was murdered. He decided he didn't need to, it felt grim to do so, sadistic almost. What good could it possibly do? He decided that no, he'd never visit that place. Never.

So instead he checked out of the hotel early and caught an overnight train to Marseille. In his cabin, which he was thankful to find empty, he opened a bottle of red wine and pulled out his diary to write. He wrote just fifteen words.

There was an explosion. Then nothing. What explosion is strong enough to destroy a world?

In Marseille he bought some cigarettes, the first time

he'd done so in over twenty-five years, a year longer than she'd even lived, then he took another train to Toulon and a bus further east along the coast. As the sun rose he caught his first glimpse of the sea and the villages which flanked it, and at last he felt at ease. He felt things were ok now, Paris was behind him, Australia was behind him, both were dead. In order for her to become alive again, he needed both to be dead. It was enough to be in the country she'd loved without being in the city that killed her. He got off the bus at a town he'd visited in his youth and photographed the street, that same first photo he snapped on this trip to France.

He entered a cafe and ordered a coffee. Eventually a short, unassuming woman with greying hair brought it to him and lazily started up a conversation.

"You're not from here, are you?" she asked in her language.

"I'm sorry," Paul said, "my French isn't so good these days, could you please speak slowly?"

"I can speak English if you'd prefer?" she offered.

"No, please, let's continue in French," Paul said, sipping his coffee, "I need the practice."

"Have you come from Paris?" she asked, taking note of his suitcase.

"I have," he answered, "and I won't be going back."

"Good idea," she said, nodding her head in agreement. "Paris is an ugly city now, it's no longer safe to walk the streets at night. My son lived there a while, but he moved home after those attacks last year. We are safer down here, and the scenery is far more beautiful."

"It certainly appears that way," Paul forced a smile. "I was here once before," he continued, "when I was much younger and presumably better looking, the town was smaller then, there were no apartment blocks, just this village surrounded by vineyards and olive groves. My whole life I've never forgotten the quality of the light here, it is unlike anywhere else I've seen. Travel fifty kilometres in either direction and it changes, it's as if there is a prism here, and when the sunlight hits it the light is somehow more magical."

The woman smiled at Paul, a genuine smile, even though she'd only understood half of what he'd said in his muddied French, then she moved along to serve another customer. Once Paul had finished his coffee he got her attention again and paid the bill.

"I'll be needing a room," he said, "until I find somewhere to settle. Do you know of anything in the village?"

"No need to explore the village," she answered, "we have five empty rooms upstairs, this season has been very slow. How long will you need it?"

"Depends on the property market, I suppose, as I'm looking to buy something down here. At least a week I'd guess."

"Follow me," she instructed, as she took a key from behind the counter and led him up some stairs. "Tomorrow you can meet my friend, Achille, he has a villa by the sea he needs to sell in a hurry. He has gambling debts from here to the moon and he'll sell it cheap!"

She switched on the light in the hallway and it flickered orange, then she unlocked a room and gestured for Paul to enter. He took one look and decided it'd be more than fine for the week.

"I'll take it," he said.

2

Paul didn't stay long in the room above the cafe, but he quickly became friends with the proprietor, Denise. Her easy manner and generosity helped Paul feel welcome in his new setting, his new life, his new corner of the world. He decided not to share his reasons for having packed up and settled there, he didn't want the sympathy, he'd had enough sympathy dumped on him to last him to the grave. But he knew that she could sense he was hurting.

One morning, as he came down for breakfast, he was surprised to find Denise seated on the customer side of the bar. She was dressed differently to how she usually was, with a pale winter frock, dark stockings, and a floral scarf over her hair, looking nothing like the barmaid Paul had come to know her as. Her eyes were hidden behind enormous yellow sunglasses, and her cheeks were glowing with rouge.

"You slept very late, Mr. Greene," she said, dangling her legs off the stool.

"Really?" he looked at his watch, "It's barely five

past nine in the morning. For someone who has literally nothing to do all day, nine's a fair effort."

"Well you've made us late," she reprimanded him, removing her sunglasses and folding them into her bag.

"I have?" he asked. "For what?"

"Achille has been waiting to take us to the villa for two hours."

"Well," Paul scratched at his chin, "it probably would've done well to have told me we had plans. You know, like last night for instance, when I said goodnight to everybody."

"I did tell you, twice. I suppose the dozen or so beers clouded your memory."

"Dozen or so, really? I could have sworn it was ten at most."

"And I could have sworn we agreed to leave at seven in the morning, now let's go," she ordered him, jumping off her stool and dragging Paul by the arm out onto the street.

Achille was a large man, with a balding head and three day growth hiding his multiple chins. His brow hung over dark, wistful eyes like a helmet, shielding the melancholy he had buried inside himself for most of his unfortunate life. He drove a beaten-up, pale blue farm truck, that looked as if it belonged in either a museum or a scrapyard. He had giant hands, textured with a symphony of scars, and forearms the width of Paul's thighs. He wore a faded blue singlet, that barely stretched out over his stomach, and his shoulders were so thick with hair it was almost impossible to know the colour of his skin beneath. He should have been a wrestler, Paul thought, he would have probably been famous.

Or he could have been a strongman at a carnival at the very least. The entire drive neither Denise nor Achille said a word, and this suited Paul fine as he got lost in his thoughts, admiring the landscape as it flew by the window like a film in fast-forward.

The drive out of town took them towards the sea, which looked to be on fire under the merciless glare of the sun. The roadside was mostly forested, until they broke out into open fields of olive trees and vineyards. There was the hint of salt lingering on the breeze, and it reminded Paul of his childhood, growing up in a small fishing village on the coast of Victoria. He felt happy, or something like happiness, for the first time he could remember, and he relaxed back into the seat and smiled. Eventually, after snaking their way down a very steep hill, they turned right off the road and onto a dirt track that descended down to the coast. Up ahead was a whitewashed stone villa, much smaller than any of the others they'd passed, surrounded by a wild, unruly garden. Achille pulled up next to the villa and stopped the truck. The three of them got out and stepped down onto the grass, still damp with morning dew and soft with swollen clay.

The scenery was perfect, Paul thought, as he made a lap of the homestead, admiring the view of the sea, the horizon and the trio of islands, like an ellipse trickling off a page. They were barely visible under the sun's haze, but already he felt a desire to visit them. Achille called him over as he unlocked the front door. Paul entered and looked around inside. It was modest and old-fashioned but full of charm. There was a small kitchen with a dining table, a living room with a desk and a couch and a small bedroom. There were plenty of windows in every room, all of which had views of the alluring sea, which shimmered and rolled like corrugated tin in the midst of summer. It was exactly what he'd hoped for, in fact far more perfect than he'd expected to find. He returned to where Achille and Denise waited, ready to make an offer.

"Well, Achille, it needs a lot of work," he said, scratching at his elbows in anticipation of a difficult sale. "It's certainly big enough for one, and the views are remarkable, but it's condition isn't great. I'd be hard pressed to have it in decent shape by summer. Firstly it needs a paint job, and it looks as if the ceiling needs work, then there's the—"

"A hundred thousand euros," Achille cut him off, his eyes fixed to the horizon, "no more, no less."

Paul was shocked, he was expecting three to four times that amount, at the very least. He didn't want Denise to think he was the type of guy to rip someone off, least of all her friend, so he tried to negotiate something higher.

"No," Achille cut him off again, "a hundred thousand euros, no more, no less. No negotiating."

Paul smiled. "If you insist, mate," he said, as Achille nodded and lumbered back to his truck.

The villa was nestled within hills tucked behind a cliff-face overlooking the Mediterranean, with torrents of waves charging like an army of foam soldiers. A constant breeze maintained a fine layer of salt on Paul's already weathered skin. It needed work, that was true, a lot of work. The walls were peeling and the floorboards were rotten in the kitchen. The garden was impenetrable in places, and made the interior feel damp and cold. The roof leaked in the bedroom and several of the shutters hung like broken limbs, but it had a kind of magic all its own.

On a fine day Paul could walk east along the cliffs through the low-lying bush, that created shelter for the native turtles and fed the wild boars at night, and down an incline to a perfectly white beach, which, apart from an abandoned cabin, seemed completely untouched by man. In the other direction were a few small neighbourhoods, not too far away, but far enough away for the villa to feel isolated. The main town centre itself was a short ride on the motorbike Paul had purchased during his second day in the village—or a long walk if he had a few too many drinks. Which was at least a few times a week.

Paul needed that feeling of isolation, it was his mission, his purpose, his nirvana. In isolation, he believed, he would find solace and eventually peace. Perhaps he'd even find forgiveness. He had isolated himself from his family, his country and even his language, which he barely used at all anymore, preferring instead to practice his French. He had isolated himself from his career, rarely checking his emails, and from his legacy, which had reached out to him several times over the past months with offers of awards and retrospectives and speaking engagements at trade shows. He rejected it all, all of it for his peaceful place by the sea.

But the sea was not peaceful in return, the sea was cruel. In fact, after a few weeks of having lived there, on several occasions it had him fearing for his life with vulgar winds that rocked the villa. Winds wild and destructive, winds which gave him the alluring, tantalising, almost life-affirming taste of death. On drunken nights alone, at his most vulnerable and most alive, he'd stand naked at the cliff's edge, gripping onto an ancient poplar tree bent almost horizontal to the earth, and would scream at the charging waves to free him of the burden of life.

"DO IT!" he'd beg. He'd collapse to his knees and cry out again. "DO IT!"

But in the morning he'd be glad to find himself still alive, glad to have had the opportunity to feel his heart race, to feel something other than hate, and especially glad to have been out of earshot of any neighbour. Yet every chance he got he'd be nude again, screaming at the wind like a madman, chasing the cocktail of life and death intermingled in the callous breath of nature. Glad, again, to wake up the next day.

One afternoon, tired of labouring away in the garden, tearing at vines and roots the strength of shipping cables, he straddled his motorbike and rode into town, weaving past the vineyards and their accompanying chateaus. He stopped by the cafe for a drink with Denise, and sat in his usual seat at the bar.

"You're exhausted again," she observed.

"I am, Denise, so how about a beer?" he asked, as he scratched at dirt in the folds of his hands.

She poured him a beer and wrote his name on a pad of paper beneath the counter. Then she drew a dash next to it.

"Working on the garden then?"

"Yes, all week. It seems no matter how much I rip it up it looks no different at the end of the day. The roots of some of those plants run the entire distance under the house, there's no getting rid of them. I'm thinking I'll just burn the lot and start over."

"I wouldn't be starting fires," Denise cautioned him, "it's been a very dry winter and your peninsula is a like a tinder-box, ready to explode."

"Is that so?" Paul asked. "Would have been nice for Achille to mention that in the sale."

"Achille is a quiet man," Denise defended her friend, "but you know I could send him down to help you out a bit? He needs a distraction every now and then."

"No," Paul rejected her offer, "the last thing I need is Achille standing there, hands on his hips like a foreman, telling me I'm doing it all wrong."

"Have it your way," she said with a shrug.

"How've you been, anyway?" Paul changed the subject. "Busy?"

"No, not busy, just the normal. The winter months are always slow here. Other businesses shut up shop and pack everything away in containers, then they live on beans and boiled rice until the summer returns. I prefer to stay open, I'd get bored otherwise. It also means I'm the only option in town if you want a beer and a decent meal. Excuse me a moment," she said, as she went to serve some construction workers, their hands black with grease, who'd come in for lunch. Paul nodded and returned to picking at his own hands.

While his French had improved a lot over the last month, he found having a conversation with Denise an exhausting exercise. Her accent was clouded by too many years of sleepless nights spent smoking in bed with strange men and her vocabulary had shrunk to what was only necessary in the bar. He assumed she'd never left the region and so she spoke a dialect that was barely recognisable as French. Yet he always resisted asking her to speak English as her English was even more painful. He enjoyed her company, though, she was vivacious and cynical in a way that made him smile, but he could sense his mood darkening and he was glad to be able to drink in peace.

In truth, it wasn't the garden which had frustrated Paul that morning, for he enjoyed the time outdoors digging up the roots and removing the weeds. It was necessary work in order to let as much sunlight into the villa as possible. The garden wasn't the issue at all. The problem was the internet.

A week earlier, despite his best instincts, Paul had contacted a local electrician to hook the villa up to the internet. It had been a frustrating affair and had cost him a small fortune, but for whatever reason he insisted on it. When he'd first bought the villa, Paul had promised himself he'd stay disconnected. The house needed too much work and there was endless nature to explore. He'd come all this way in order to think, in order to breathe, in order to just be. To cook, fish, climb mountains, swim in the nude, get shitfaced and scream against the wind—it didn't matter—just be. But the truth was he was already bored, he was lonely and he wanted to connect.

When he first logged on, after weeks of silence, there was not much correspondence and it gave him a deflating feeling of irrelevance. He realised, for the first time in his life, that the world would keep on spinning no matter what became of him. Paul Greene could vanish tomorrow and no one would care, possibly no one would even notice. Once a famously brave photographer, headhunted by Magnum and everyone else who mattered, Paul had, in recent years, faded into obscurity as his own agency struggled to adapt to modern technologies. But then some emails started to trickle through, from lawyers, accountants, debt-collectors, the usual junk, and he felt just a tiny bit relevant again. He ignored them all, of course he did—they couldn't touch him in France, their laws didn't matter over here. With his dual British passport he was basically a French citizen, and those leeches in Australia would have to starve waiting for his blood. He was immune to them, but on that particular morning an email had come through from someone he wasn't immune to; his ex-wife.

Eight months earlier, when news came through that his daughter, Vanessa, might have been caught up in a terrorist attack in Paris, Paul was at home. He'd gotten dressed that morning, his normal routine of showering, shaving, selecting a shirt and trousers, and went downstairs and made breakfast. Then he switched on the news. Four bombs had gone off in the Parisian metro, and several dozen people were feared dead. Straight away he reached for his phone and called Vanessa's number—it rang out. He checked her social media, she hadn't been online all day. He knew for sure she was safe, she had to be, how many million people were there in Paris? There was no way she was caught up in it, that kind of thing happened to other people, not him and definitely not his daughter. But something in his gut didn't sit right. Something felt wrong.

He yelled upstairs to his wife, Angelica, but she was preoccupied with a presentation she was to give at work that morning, rehearsing it in front of the mirror in their bedroom, and she ignored him. If all went well she was in line for a massive promotion and she was too busy for Paul. He rushed up to her.

"Ange, there's been another attack in Paris," he told her, surprised to find himself stuttering.

"Oh dear," she groaned, "how terrible. They're just such an easy target, the French, letting in all those refugees."

"Vanessa isn't picking up her phone!" he cried, dialling her number again.

"Really? What's the time there? She's probably just asleep."

"It's 10pm," Paul replied, "she's not asleep. She's not fucking asleep."

"I need you to relax Paul," she demanded, as she turned away from the mirror and glared at him. "You're stressing me out and you know that today is too important for this shit."

"Stressing you out?" he shouted at her, stunned. "My concern for our daughter's safety is stressing you out? She could be dead."

"Your daughter, Paul!" she snapped. "Your fucking daughter! Now I need to fucking rehearse this before I leave for work! Get out!"

With those words Paul knew it didn't matter what had happened to Vanessa, Angelica was finished. It was true, she wasn't Vanessa's mother, that was Rebecca, who'd succumbed to cancer when Vanessa was just nine years old. But Paul had been married to Angelica for over five years now, and it was an unforgivable thing for her to say.

When it became apparent, later that evening, via the Australian consulate in Paris, that Vanessa had most likely been killed in the attack, riding the Paris metro line number 3, Paul was laying on the floor of his brother's kitchen. He was shocked to find that he didn't cry, he didn't scream or sob or curse the world, he just stared at the ceiling, while those around him, his brother and his brother's wife and his niece and his nephew, pulled at his limbs, drenched him with their tears, cluttered his thoughts with their shrieks and their wails and their thumping on the tiles. Paul remained perfectly still. He didn't make a sound.

A couple of hours later, Angelica began calling his phone so incessantly that Paul climbed to his feet and threw it off the balcony. When she turned up at his brother's apartment building later that night to see if he was there, Paul informed her from above that it was over, that it was done, and he called her "a rotten bitch who can't even fuck properly." He wasn't sure why he'd said that. He was embarrassed when it was repeated in court. He guessed he'd just felt like hurting her somehow, like she'd hurt him earlier that morning.

She took everything she could, leaving Paul just enough to die on, as his accountant had said, and now she'd emailed him to see if he was ok. It had ruined Paul's day.

"Denise," he called across the bar, "another when you're ready."

Denise grabbed a chilled glass from the fridge and poured Paul another beer, she pulled out her pad to scribble down another dash next to his name when a voice stopped her, a voice both her and Paul recognised immediately. It was not a voice one could ever forget.

"Don't charge that one, Denny, it's on me. And what the hell? Make it two, would you?"

Paul swung around on his stool, and couldn't quite believe who was standing in front of him.

"Don't get up, Paul," the man said, dragging another stool over to the bar, "let me join you, back in our natural habitat. Nice to see you're not dead after all these years."

"Raymond Bishop," Paul gasped, gripping the shoulder of the man who was now seated beside him, he was surprised to find his muscles still strong, still athletic. "What on earth are you doing here?"

"I'm surprised you can even recognise me under the beard," he laughed, as he packed tobacco into his wooden pipe, "I've tried to go incognito, y'know, too many debts I can't be bothered paying."

"It's the voice, Raymond, good luck trying to disguise that. I've known plenty of Scotsmen in my life, but none took the mickey out of the accent quite like you."

"Like Sean Connery drowning in a vat of whisky, you once said."

"Nice to see your memory isn't shot."

"It's the final piece of me that works. Denny, love," Raymond called across the bar, "we'll be needing two whiskies to go with these beers, you know the brand."

Denise reached for a bottle and poured the drinks.

"Honestly, why the hell are you here, Raymond? I thought for sure this was a corner of the world where I could disappear without running into old sparring partners, especially ones who ought to be six feet under by now."

"I live here Paul, this is my home. I've been here twenty years or more and I still only speak three words of French, *parlez vous anglais?* It's a horrid language, really, should have been forsaken when the Yanks liberated Paris."

"You haven't changed a bit," Paul laughed.

"Six wives have tried and six wives have walked away millionaires. Speaking of wives, where's yours?"

"You mean Rebecca?"

"Who else?"

Paul went silent for a moment, Rebecca and Raymond had a history together, and Paul had never thought to call Raymond and tell him of her death, all those years ago.

"She passed away actually, it's been fifteen years now. I'm sorry Raymond, I should have contacted you somehow, she was always fond of you. After that I married again, a long time after, but that has finished as well, some men just aren't cut out for it I guess."

"Sorry to hear that Paul, Rebecca was a marvellous woman, truly one of the greats. Let's drink to her, then. Denny, two more," Raymond called across the bar as he lit his pipe and took a puff. "You know, when I began hearing there was an Australian photographer in town, pushing 60 but still handsome enough to start rumours, roaring up and down the coast on his motorbike at all hours of the night, I had no doubt who it was. And then I heard you bought that dump off Achille out on the cliffs? Tell me it ain't so, that thing will cause you a lifetime of pain."

"Well, if anyone knows pain, Raymond, it's you. You were a foreign correspondent in the seventies, after all.

Few lives have been quite so dramatic."

"What choice did I have?" Raymond shrugged. "Adventure was my mistress."

"And what were your actual mistresses then?"

"Just a way to keep warm," Raymond shrugged, "nothing more. Denny, another!" he shouted at the barmaid.

3

The first of March was a famous day in the region, for the doldrum of winter had been outlasted and life could begin to trickle back into the villages with the first redeeming rays of springtime sun. For a short while the locals were allowed to enjoy the place to themselves, before the regrettable hoards of summer tourists flooded in by June. Raymond had insisted Paul keep the day free and he turned up at his villa at eleven in the morning, driving a red convertible Corvette.

"What year's she dated?" Paul asked, as Raymond, wearing a navy sports jacket with white linen trousers and a red silk cravat, leapt out of the car. His height and nimbleness made him appear a much younger man than seventy-eight.

"Damned if I know," he replied, "I've never cared a thing for cars and therefore, such is the way with life, I've never gone a day without a knockout."

"There'd be people over in Saint-Tropez who'd cut off a limb to drive something like this," Paul continued, running his hand along the curve of the fender, careful not to leave a mark.

"Over in Saint-Tropez they hack away their limbs for just about anything," Raymond groaned, "it's their national sport. A glimpse of Brigitte Bardot's raw ass goes for two legs and a forearm. I, on the other hand, would be sitting in the corner hacking off my own legs, begging her to put her pants back on."

"Not a fan I take it Raymond?"

"Not anymore," Raymond sniped, as he walked past Paul and down towards the villa. "I fell out of love with her long ago. Now she's just another racist, and France has plenty of those already."

Paul gave him an uneasy smile, for he'd read some of her writing just recently and he'd agreed with almost everything she'd written.

"I mean," he started, "it's hard to disagree that Arabs are changing France. And not necessarily for the better."

Raymond threw Paul a look, an interrogating look, "So, you're one of them too, then?" he asked.

Paul decided not to answer. "This way," he said, changing the conversation, "let me show you around."

Paul had spent the previous two weeks clearing out the vines that entangled the villa like a nest of serpents. For the first time from the driveway one could see all the way down past the villa out to sea. The sea was languid, like a fading hangover, and Paul felt the sudden urge to swim.

"This place is a dump, Paul," Raymond cautioned his friend, as he kicked at loose stones in the muddied turf. "You want to borrow some cash? I've got more than I'm ever going to need, you could purchase yourself something liveable, far away from this rotten lake."

"I'm fine, Raymond, I've got enough. Besides this lake has charm, you just need the right kind of eyes to see it."

"Had charm, maybe, just like Bardot."

"I have plans to fix it all up a bit, it mostly just needs a coat of paint. It's going to take me months, though," Paul admitted.

"Well, do me a favour and get dressed first would you? We don't have all day," he went on, "I've got a surprise waiting, two of 'em, actually. I'll meet you back at the car."

The drive from Paul's villa took them away from the sea and wound its way like a racetrack. Eventually they left the neighbourhoods behind and sped through miles of rolling vineyards, each with elegant, imposing chateaus at the end of grand old driveways. Driveways lined with poplar trees and guarded by well-baited dobermans. Raymond made a right and climbed a steep hill, forested now, as the sunlight dappled the windscreen through the thin canopy of oak trees, still recovering from the winter drought.

Paul felt happy again, he always did on drives around the hinterland. He turned and smiled at Raymond, as the wind swept his brilliant silver-blonde hair from his forehead like a banner in a storm.

"Thank you, Raymond, I needed this," he said.

Raymond smirked and hit the gas even harder as they sped past a disused windmill, "Don't thank me yet Paul, the fun hasn't even started."

Ramatuelle was a medieval village on a hill, a legendary one in a region full of them. It was a stone village mostly, with wooden finishes conjuring up goblins, gnomes and faeries. Around every corner were startling flourishes of colour made possible from flowering bougainvillea and eccentric window frames. The doors were cracked and ancient, while the streets were narrow cobblestoned mazes, not out of place in a Moroccan fantasy.

"These hill-top towns were built to escape the pirates who once terrorised Saint-Tropez," Raymond explained. "Now they're mostly empty outside the tourist season, except for bastards like us, wealthy enough to dine here even in the winter months."

What made Ramatuelle different to the other towns were the sweeping views across Plage de Pampelonne, the longest and most sought after beach in the region. The jewel in the crown of the Var.

Raymond ushered Paul into a restaurant across the street from where he'd parked. "Let's have a few drinks before they arrive," he said, as he held the door for Paul.

"We're expecting company then, I take it?" Paul asked.

"It wouldn't be the first day of spring if love weren't in the air," Raymond laughed.

As they entered the restaurant the manager, a short, dark, muscular man with an Italian accent and no older than thirty five, came to greet Raymond.

"Bello! Bello!" he cried, gripping Raymond's blushing cheeks as he reached up on his toes to kiss each one. "Once again you are my very first booking for the season, and as always the best looking. I have put a bottle of Krug on ice for you, on me of course."

"Cheers, Al. Look, I'd like you to meet my friend

Paul, I've known him since we did assignments together in Africa in the early eighties, he's one of the last true photographers left."

"Nice to meet you," Paul said, shaking the manager's hand, "don't listen to him though, I haven't taken a decent photo in fifteen years."

Al lead Paul and Raymond to the bar as he went behind to prepare them some drinks. Raymond, as always, led the conversation.

"I remember it well, it was 1982, we were doing a piece on the conservation of African elephants for Life magazine. Paul would take a few snaps and I'd write eight or so thousand words, a standard editorial back then. We'd been there two months, somewhere in the back country of Nigeria, and Paul had taken a real liking to one particular elephant. What'd we call him?" he asked, turning to Paul.

"Elvis," Paul answered, "he was pretty damn fat."

"That's right," Raymond laughed, "even for an elephant this thing was fat. Then one evening, as Paul and I were getting cozy with a few Ethiopian girls we'd met on the plane, Elvis rocks up to the camp and starts huffing and puffing and stomping around like a fool. I was shit scared of losing the girls, who in turn were shit scared of the damn elephant, and so I sent Paul over to calm him down. Next thing you know Paul has a tusk through his shoulder and is on his way to hospital."

"That's not quite how it happened," Paul interrupted.

"Oh bullshit," Raymond countered him, "that's always how it happened Paul—you were the saint on his way to the hospital while I was promising the girls back in the tent I had more than enough stamina to last the night. And once or twice I did!"

"Raymond was like a mentor to me," Paul moved on, "taught me all the intricacies and secrecies of being a foreign correspondent. Like how to do favours for the locals in return for information—or photographs. He was my big brother and then one evening, just like that, he vanished, I barely saw him again. Until now."

The two of them were silent a moment, as the young manager glanced between them, unsure of why the mood had changed.

Then suddenly the door opened behind them and the tension evaporated, as two middle-aged women walked into the room and the tiny restaurant was flooded with light. Raymond wiped his mouth and sprung to his feet.

"Susana, Margaret," he bellowed, kissing them each on the cheek as Al took their coats and hung them behind the bar. "Please, make acquaintance with my dear friend Paul, a friend of mine from a time when men could be men and women could be women."

Paul stood up and straightened his belt and trousers, already feeling drunk after the cocktails Al had fed him.

"Pleasure to meet you," he said, reaching out his hand to shake each of theirs. They laughed and ignored his handshake and instead kissed each of his cheeks.

The four of them were the only guests at Al's that afternoon, no one else even stopped by to poke their head in. Raymond organised the menu and Al took care of all the drinks while Paul, relaxed in the corner of the booth, felt weightless in a dreamy, soft afternoon drunkenness. Outside it looked like it could rain.

"So, you went through Africa together, what else?" Margaret asked, her glass of red wine almost horizontal to the table as she balanced it with uneasy fingers, her words slurring to the point where Raymond was easier to understand.

"I'm pretty sure that was all," Raymond answered, raising an eyebrow at Paul, "I mean, we ran into one another now and then, in London, New York, Rome, but that was our only job together, no?"

"No," Paul replied, looking up from his glass, "it wasn't."

"Really?" Raymond challenged him, "I thought my memory served me well enough."

"I'm sure it does, Ray, when you want to remember something, but when you don't…" Paul taunted.

"Oh, not this," Raymond blurted out, splashing red wine onto his linen trousers, "I thought for sure you were over this!"

"Over what?" Susana asked, one arm around Paul's shoulder while the other reached for her glass of chardonnay. "Sounds juicy."

"It's nothing, I shouldn't have said anything," Paul apologised.

"Oh, stop being a bore and tell us," Margaret demanded, now seated on Raymond's lap, one hand tickling his thigh under the table, "you're putting us to sleep Paul, really you are!"

"Ok, fine," Paul gave in, "it was New York, 1983. I was stationed there working for Vogue, they gave me an assignment photographing a party at one of Robert Maxwell's mansions. My date that night was a model, her name was Rebecca Livingston and she was a total knockout, the kind of woman who'd take the breath out of the entire room with the flutter of her eyelashes. No one else even existed when she entered a space." He drifted off for a moment as he reached for his whisky. "No one," he continued.

"Go on," Susana chided him, "I want to see how I compare to this Rebecca, she sounds hot."

"You don't," Paul muttered, his own words slurring now, "no one ever did, and no one ever will."

"Ouch," Margaret grinned. "I still don't understand the point of this story, though, I thought this was about the two of you?" she asked, as she tilted her head towards Raymond.

"It is about us," Paul continued. "The story, I suppose, is that Raymond happened to be there that night too, working on the same event, the same magazine and predictably—the same girl."

"Alright, enough!" Raymond cut his story short, slamming his glass down on the table. "The story ends exactly how you all imagine it does, let's not ruin the party by spelling it out."

"I agree," Paul said, his head downcast, "let's not spoil another evening."

"Al!" Raymond called across the room. "How about you pop that bottle of Dom Perin—whatever the hell it was! This wedding's about to become a funeral."

Al did as he was ordered and emptied the bottle of Krug into four champagne flutes, while Margaret, now completely smashed, toasted the first day of spring, as Susana made Paul a quiet offer.

"Follow me," she whispered as she climbed uneasily to her feet. He did.

As Paul and Susana climbed the narrow staircase up towards the bathroom she gripped his hand tightly and turned around to smile at him.

"Promise me something," she cooed in his ear.

"Promise what?" he asked as she kissed him on the lips.

"You won't say a thing to Margaret."

"Of course I won't, but something tells me she wouldn't care," he said as he glanced over the railing at Margaret and Raymond below, locked in a passionate embrace of their own.

"Not about us silly, about this," she giggled as she produced two pills in the palm of her hand.

"What the hell is this?" Paul demanded.

"Shhh," she quieted him, as she put her hand over his mouth, "it's ecstasy, my son sends it over from England. Don't worry handsome, it's a beginner's dose."

"I think I'd rather not," Paul declined, pushing her hand away.

"Why, you don't like me?" she asked.

"I do, of course, I mean, why not? I just haven't done ecstasy before and I'm not sure this is the time. When did lunch and a few drinks stop being enough?"

"Just kiss me darling," she begged, "just another kiss."

As Paul kissed her he felt the pill slip out of her mouth and into his own, and instead of fighting it he just kissed her harder and washed it down with her saliva. She dragged him into the bathroom and started to loosen her dress while Paul undid his belt and lowered his trousers.

"Fuck me," she whispered in his ear.

"I will," he reassured her as he struggled with his underwear, "just give me a second."

"Fuck me like I'm Rebecca," she begged him.

"What?" Paul asked, pulling away, unsure if he'd heard her correctly.

"I said, fuck me like I'm Rebecca. She sounded hot."

Paul paused a moment and made eye contact with himself in the mirror. Already his pupils were widening and his pulse was charging like a thoroughbred on the sprint. Beads of sweat raced down his forehead. What had he become? He swallowed a hard breath and forced a smile, it was a sad, pathetic smile, but it was all he could muster, and it'd have to be enough.

"Ok," he said as he entered her, "Rebecca."

4

Paul woke up in agony, his head thumping away like a drum solo. He didn't know where he was. He flicked his eyes around the room, trying to recognise anything, trying to place himself, but the slightest movement caused insufferable pain, like electric shots shooting through his skull, and he retreated into the dark. Eventually, after several minutes of stillness, he worked up the courage and reached around the bed, or was it a couch, and searched for a glass of water. It was useless, there wasn't one, there was nothing to help ease him back to life. He let out a groan as he lowered his head back down and brought a pillow over his face, a futile effort to drown out the light streaking in from the balcony doors.

"What happened last night?" he muttered to himself, barely audible through the pillow.

As he laid there, unable to get up and unable to sleep, he tried his best to piece the previous evening together. He remembered the lunch, lamb cutlets to start and duck breast to finish, and he remembered the women, Susana with her London twang and blonde curls and Margaret with her mid-Atlantic drawl and jet-black bob. How did Raymond know them again? Who cares, he decided, he didn't expect to keep acquaintance with them anyway. He certainly hoped he wouldn't. Then slowly he began to remember his rendezvous in the bathroom with Susana and the pill she gave him. It came back to him like the broken sequence of a dream. No wonder his head hurt so damn much, no wonder the whole night was muddled in his memory. He called her Rebecca, didn't he? Goddamnit! Why the hell did he do that? What was that strange kink of hers? What kind of morbid shit storm had his life become?

"Sorry, Rebecca," he whispered, cowering under the pillow.

After their tryst in the bathroom they'd rejoined Raymond and Margaret at the table and by then Al had joined them too. He remembered Al getting up and locking the restaurant's door, just to be sure no one else would interfere, then Susana got out more of those pills and she crushed them up and sprinkled them into their drinks, without anyone but Paul noticing. Who was this woman? At some point Raymond cornered him in a booth and tried to apologise for what had happened years ago, and then he reprimanded Paul for not telling him about Rebecca dying. What the hell, Paul thought, he'd been the last person on his mind that week. That week had been torture, the worst of his life, second worst maybe, and he still wasn't over it. How dare Raymond make it about him.

Paul tossed the pillow away and managed to sit up, he thrust his legs off the couch and sat still a moment, focusing on a corner of the coffee table to steady his vision. He could smell himself and he smelt awful.

"I'm too old for this shit," he said.

After a short while he looked up, he was in a living room, haphazardly decorated with old world colonial charm. It had to be Raymond's living room, he figured. High up on the wall opposite him, above a fireplace, was a rhino's head. Some kind of hunting trophy, he guessed, surrounded by a seemingly endless array of antlers. Under it on the mantel was a stuffed jungle cat, larger than a house cat but much smaller than a regular jungle cat, probably a cub he assumed. So, Raymond shot animals. The man who loved the wilds of Africa more dearly than anything else life had offered him, went out and murdered it. Made sense, Paul decided. Raymond was, after all, a living, breathing mess of contradictions.

As he climbed to his feet he was relieved to find his headache had faded a little, and on the stand behind the couch there was, to his relief, a large glass of water. He drank it down in a single effort, then Paul went over to the balcony doors and looked outside. It was a cold day, and a light rain cooled Raymond's garden, which was not so unlike the jungles of the Congo where the two of them had travelled together once, photographing gorillas, as they journeyed down the rivers to meet a tribal chieftain. Paul went outside and sat on a cane rocking chair. He found enough inner peace to relax for a moment, as he scanned the palms for bird life.

The nature surrounding him, which smelled of moistened earth and peeling moss had, for a moment, helped him feel ok, but then as suddenly as a bolt of light from a storm, a profound sadness washed over him. He felt he'd betrayed Rebecca the previous evening. He'd treated her like dirt, like nothing more than an anecdote at the bottom of a martini. The girls had depressed him, Raymond too, and the whole evening had been one to regret.

He missed Rebecca, as deeply as he'd ever missed anything in his life. He remembered what it was like getting drunk with her, it was fun, always fun. Like he'd done with Susana, he'd made drunken love to Rebecca in bathrooms too, at parties, clubs, once even at a soiree at the White House when John Travolta danced with Princess Diana. He'd had his photo taken with Clint Eastwood that night, and not long after he had to rush Rebecca back to the hotel after she started vomiting in the Rose Garden. Rebecca had been free, mad even, and he was at his best when she'd been beside him.

He missed her, too much, and Vanessa too. His life without them had become a farce, a complete mockery, and he didn't know what, if anything he could do to change it. He didn't know if he wanted to change it. Without the two women he loved, he may as well burn out as brightly as possible, throw caution to the wind, vanish out of view. Let Raymond destroy him like he'd destroyed the rhino and the jungle cat and those animals who'd once owned the antlers.

Raymond was a good enough man, Paul thought, but he was a brute and intimidating and always had to have his own way. Raymond was old-school, the new world didn't suit him, so he lived away from it all, as secluded as possible, in his mansion in the jungle. He was fun though, and when there was nothing much to look forward to, having Raymond around was useful.

The wind carried the light rain horizontally now, and it started to reach the rocking chair. Paul got up and went inside to stay dry, when he noticed a picture of himself and Raymond on the wall. It was black and white, with Raymond standing on the right, dressed in a loose linen shirt and safari trousers, while Paul, squatting next to him, had a cigarette dangling between his lips and a camera in his hands. Behind them was an enormous African elephant, probably Elvis, Paul figured. They were handsome back then, roguish, successful, the luckiest men on the planet. Living a life right out of great literature. Paul pulled out his phone and took a photo of the photo, as he heard Raymond enter the living room behind him.

"Glad to see you're alive," he said.

"If this is alive, do me a favour and take one of those guns off the wall and finish me off," Paul pleaded, his headache flaring with every syllable.

"How was your night then? I was happy to see you and Susana hit it off, she can be hard to please."

"Really?" Paul asked. "I'd barely opened my mouth before she'd opened her legs."

"She's a go-getter, she knows what she wants and she gets it."

"I shouldn't have let anything happen, Raymond, I have no interest in her," Paul admitted.

"Relax Paul, she's got a husband. She won't be bothering you anytime soon," he reassured his friend.

"Excuse me?" Paul blurted out.

"Oh come on, you think a single woman would let

herself have that much fun? They're both married, of course they are, to men they don't care for, but men they can't be bothered leaving. Divorce is a hell of a pain in the ass, you ought to know as well as anyone. Each side allows the other to play up, then when the evening calls for it, they play happy couples in front of the cameras."

"Sounds like hell," Paul muttered.

"You didn't think it was hell last night," Raymond laughed.

"I didn't think much of anything last night," Paul uttered, before changing the subject. "It's a nice house you have here, Ray, it's as if your biography jumped off the page and manifested itself as furniture and plants and trinkets from a long forgotten war. The war of life. I was sitting out there on the balcony just now, and I could have sworn I was back in Africa."

"Some men never leave a place, Paul. I don't know about you, but I was never happier than when I was in the shadow of Kilimanjaro."

"That rhino over there," Paul said, gesturing to the head on the wall, "is it real?"

"As real as the bastard who shot it," Raymond answered. "It was a different time, I'm not proud of it, but the poor beast is dead, so I may as well show him off."

"They're probably extinct by now," Paul mused.

"Probably, and if they're not they're like us, the last of a wild breed not long left for this world."

"We're not that old, Raymond," Paul reassured his friend. Although, deep down he felt the weight of his fifty-eight years as heavily as ever.

"You may not be, but seventy-eight is old in any language and I feel it in my bones more every day. Especially the bone that matters, as Margaret discovered last night." Raymond slapped Paul on the shoulder and turned to face the balcony. "This is the first rain I've seen in months, but it's not going to be enough to hold off catastrophe out in those forests. One bad storm and the whole coast will go up."

"Is it really that dire?" Paul asked.

Raymond grunted. "It has the potential to be, we'll see if this rain can hold. You need a lift back to the villa? I'm heading into town in ten minutes," Raymond offered as he turned away and exited the room. "I'll be happy to take you," he called behind him.

"Coming," Paul replied, as he glanced back at the photo once more.

The rest of the day Paul spent trying to sleep, tossing and turning with uneasy memories of his wife and daughter. He recalled the last conversation he'd had with Vanessa, cancelling the plans they'd made to spend Christmas together in Greece because Angelica didn't like the idea of being so close to the refugee camps. He recalled the aftermath of the attacks that took his daughter, the vitriol in the newspapers, the hate which spewed out on cable television. There was a hashtag, a march, a protest, an assassination attempt on the French President. Paul hid from it all and tried to run his agency as best he could, until he just gave up. It was pointless, he'd become a nihilist, he cared for nothing. He still turned up at the office, but his responsibilities were slowly chipped away at by his colleagues, by people he'd hired, trained himself. People he'd given a break to in an industry impossible to crack.

They had babied him, tolerated him, how could they not? The trauma was very real, and after a while Paul wasn't much more than a ghost. His colleagues were never sure he wouldn't kill himself at any moment.

He lost weight, friends, money. When he told his brother he was moving to France his brother told him he was mad. They had a huge argument and his brother only backed down when Paul made it clear there were only two options, France or death. Perhaps they would end up being the same thing, but he thought it was worth trying the former first.

At eight o'clock, before it was too dark, he climbed out of his bed and looked out the window. The rain had died away and the clouds had parted just enough to let a little light through. The sea looked still and warm, as it always did after a rain, and the seabirds fought for position over schools of fish that foolishly flirted with the surface. He grabbed a bottle of wine from his kitchen and walked down the path, away from the villa and towards the sand.

As he walked he counted the seconds between the rotation of the lighthouse out on the island, which had only just flared up, and then he counted the cargo ships, isolated from one another along the lonesome axis of the horizon. When he arrived at the beach he took a healthy swig of wine and planted the bottle next to him, then he removed his jacket, his trousers, shirt, shoes and underwear, and standing naked on the shoreline he noticed the first star.

The water was warm, warmer than the air above it, and he dived under, eyes-wide open. Momentarily he felt alive. Floating on his back he decided against feeling guilty for the moment spent with Susana. They were two adults having fun, what of it, no-one was harmed. Then he managed to turn his mind to silence, something he hadn't done in years, and he remained like that as the last mad dash of sunlight flitted away from the coast like a dove.

Sometime later, an hour, maybe two, he collected his clothes in the dark and returned to the villa in the nude. Once inside he showered and dried himself off, then he opened his laptop for the first time that week and logged on to his email. He emptied the remainder of the wine into a glass and took a swig. There were the usual emails from debt collectors and accountants, splattered amongst mountains of junk. He deleted the lot without a second thought.

"What a load of shit," he muttered.

But as he was about to log off for the evening he noticed an email from a name he didn't recognise—someone named Samia.

He opened it, and it read:

Mr. Greene,

I'm sorry to bother you, but I need to reach out. I was a friend of your daughter, Vanessa, a close friend. I found your email on your agency website, Vanessa spoke of you often and showed me your work. I thought it was very beautiful, and I remembered it. I hope you don't mind.

I miss Vanessa, too much, and I would like to talk to someone who knew her, knew her well like I did. It's unlikely, but if you're ever in France, please visit me in Paris. I could show you where we lived together for a short time. I could show you her favourite cafes

Paul closed the laptop and sat back in his chair. Part of him worried the email was some kind of sophisticated scam, the type that plays to a man's weakest sensibilities—loss, suffering, broken-heartedness—and then exploits them. But at the same time he was too curious to let it go. What if this person had been sent to him for a reason? What if she were sent to save him? She could tell him about Vanessa's last months. What Vanessa had looked like, if she had been happy, if she had been in love.

He decided the only thing would be to sleep on it and make a decision to reply or not in the morning. And so he finished his glass of wine, undressed and climbed into bed, but he could not sleep. Instead he laid there, counting the rotations of the lighthouse. By the time he'd counted two hundred and forty, he realised he'd been laying there for two hours, wide awake. So he got up, he opened his laptop and he wrote a reply.

He signed it off with:

5

The train station in Toulon was alive with commotion, which made Paul, now accustomed to the tranquility of the village and especially the villa, feel both uneasy and excited at the same time. He sat in a cafe attached to the arrival hall, already on his second coffee, as he basked in the morning light that flooded the space from enormous arched windows. Behind the windows were the mountains, silver grey, and behind the mountains the rest of France sprawled out like a constellation of broken hearts.

Outside the cafe were businessmen and women, dressed mostly in black, smoking the day's first or fifth cigarette, already oppressed by phone conferences with managers and partners and executives. Their French, barely pronounced, added to the erratic symphony of the station's ambience. They looked enslaved, Paul thought, as if they'd lost their will in some pact with the devil. He was glad to be free at last of any kind of professional duty. Free from the man. Rising above them was the song of a communal piano, suffering through an ill-attempted sonata, and the shouts of protesters demanding shorter working weeks and higher wages. There was the bickering and squabbling of Roma children and their parents as they split a loaf of bread for breakfast, and the unbearable honking of taxis as they fought one another for the scraps of passengers arriving off the 8:15 from Paris. In truth, he was more uneasy than excited.

It was the 9:15 from Paris Paul was there to greet. He'd spent the entire night prior tossing and turning in bed, and decided to hit the road early and take the drive in Raymond's red convertible, which he'd borrowed, as slowly as possible. But he was anxious, and in his anxiety he sped the entire way. He roared along the coast past the town of Cavalaire-sur Mer, with its harbour-side brasseries waking up slowly with the sun. Through Le Lavandou with its enormous beach laying in wait for the hoards of June tourists. And straight through Hyeres, with its infantry of brilliant African palms standing as sentinels at the gates of Toulon. Now he sat in the cafe, another hour to kill, about to order his third coffee for the morning. He glanced at the mountains—the rearguard of the city—as they sparkled in the light like shores of diamonds.

Paul was certain he'd done something dumb, something he'd regret. He had, over the past months in the villa, managed to forget Vanessa somewhat. He hadn't told anyone what had happened. Not Raymond, nor Denise, nor Achille. He hadn't even told them she'd existed at all. He'd kept it hidden, tucked away like a former identity killed off in a fake yachting accident. It hurt him to admit it, but he'd washed himself clean of her, and he preferred it that way.

It's not what Vanessa deserved, of course not, but it was what Paul needed—or what he thought he needed. There could be no rejuvenating ocean swims, no pleasant strolls through Sunday markets, no exhilarating rides along winding mountain roads on his motorbike if he was too caught up in the death of his daughter. He couldn't allow himself to become too distraught in her memory, in the visions of her auburn hair and pixie nose, her eyes like her mothers and her lips like his. Her laughter, like a drug. Never a moment went by without him yearning for her. So he blocked her out, what choice did he have?

Paul shook the memory of Vanessa and glanced up from his table. He looked outside the cafe again and now, as if out of no where, all he could notice were crowds of Arabs. And he wanted them to disappear. He wanted them to leave. He didn't want to hate them, but their hate had taken his daughter, or so he told himself, and therefore he had little choice but to return it. What was it with these people that made them so violent, he wondered. Was he even safe here, waiting for his coffee? How could anyone know when the next bomb was to go off? No one was safe, ever.

Was he becoming racist? he wondered, as the waiter brought over another cappuccino. He'd never been racist before, he'd never spent five minutes thinking about the idea of race. It hadn't occurred to him that people might be made differently. He'd spent most of his life travelling, through Asia, Africa, Europe, the Americas. It was his job, his livelihood, his vocation, to capture truth and suffering and the essence of life through his lens. He'd had such a powerful empathy with his subjects that he'd been the most famous photographer in the world once, even for a time being the personal photographer of the President of the United States. He was a man of the world, an international, a citizen without borders. He'd known Arabs before, plenty of them, and they were wonderful people who he'd loved very much. But maybe they were the exception—not the rule, he thought.

After the explosion he was encouraged by his psychiatrist to join an online forum with other grieving family members—sons, daughters, mothers—who'd lost someone in similar attacks. They'd opened his eyes to things he never could have known. They spoke about how Arab women couldn't leave the home, that they were married off as children, that they were dirty, unwashed people whose religion was only interested in war and murder. They obsessed over genital mutilation, over harems of unconsenting teenage girls, over beheadings in public squares and unnatural relationships with animals. They told him that the only goal of the Arab was the reconquest of the West and the enslavement of women. He thought it was all rubbish at first, of course he did, but he kept reading because he didn't know where else to turn, and the longer he stayed logged in to these forums the more he stopped dismissing the ideas. But at least he wasn't like Angelica, he thought, who had once gone up and spat in the face of an Arab woman because she was making silly faces at a blonde child in a supermarket. At least he wasn't extreme like his ex-wife, he reassured himself.

He finished off his coffee and paid his bill. He still

had forty-five minutes to wait but he no longer felt safe at the station, so he decided to go for a walk. He made his way from the station down towards the city, past the opera house and into the narrow alleyways, barely wide enough for a car to scrape through. Eventually he could see the shimmering light of the harbour and he went and sat along its promenade. He was tired and his eyes felt like closing, but he didn't allow himself a moment's rest, lest he slept too long and forgot to pick her up. Again he remonstrated himself, what madness had led him to invite this stranger, this young girl, into his home for the whole month of May. What good could come of it?

What if he just left? he thought. What if he sent her a text to collect an envelope from the cafe, in which he'd leave a hundred euros and a note apologising for wasting her time? He'd tell her to buy herself lunch, return to Paris and not contact him again. He'd tell her to just forget Vanessa, as he had done. He'd tell her it was in her best interest, he'd tell her it was the only way of moving on. It's what Vanessa would want. Vanessa is dead, he'd say, and by you coming here to meet me we're bringing her back to life. Leave the dead be you stupid girl.

He looked at his watch—it was five past nine and the train was arriving in ten minutes. As he hurried back to the station he stopped to catch his breath and looked himself over in the reflection of a storefront window—he'd put on weight, not a lot but a noticeable amount. It suited him, he thought, he'd always been too thin. Besides, what was France if not cheese and wine and bread? He ran in his fingers through his hair and straightened his sunglasses, then he patted down his facial hair which was somewhere between stubble and a light beard. He made himself look as good as he possibly could for the girl. But why? Then he rushed to meet her where they'd arranged, out the front of the newsagent near the station entrance.

As he entered the station an announcement told him her train was just arriving. The place was busier now, more crowded. The protest outside had grown in both size and volume and there were dozens of children rushing through the hall to get the train to school. There was a heavy police presence, as was the case at every train station in France. There were even military men with enormous rifles stationed at strategic spots. Thankfully, at least, no one had thought to play the damned piano.

Suddenly crowds began spilling out of platform one, and Paul looked around for any sign of Samia. He had no idea what she would look like, just that she'd be wearing a red sweater. After five or so minutes the crowd trickled down to just a few people, but there was still no sign of her. He pulled out his phone and dialled her number.

"Hello," he said as she answered, "it's Paul."

"Yes, I know, your name came up when you called."

"Sorry, of course. I'm just out the front of the newsagent, as we agreed, but I can't see any red sweaters. Did you make it to Toulon ok?"

"Of course there are no red sweaters, it's not the fashion," she laughed. "It was you, Paul, who said you'd wear the red sweater, not me."

"Oh shit, shit, you're right," he said, as he cursed

his fading memory, "I'm really sorry. And sorry for swearing, shit."

She laughed again.

"So where are you then?" he asked, scanning the platform exit.

"Out the front of the newsagents, where we agreed to meet, behind you actually."

Paul turned around as he lowered his phone and there she stood, right behind him as she'd said. She was wearing all black—black leather shoes, black jeans and a black singlet top. Her hair was black too, and her skin a light shade of brown. Two things struck Paul, as he looked at her for the first time. Firstly, she was beautiful, very beautiful, more beautiful than any woman he'd seen in a long time. And secondly, she was an Arab.

6

On the drive back along the coast towards the village, Paul was uneasy. He felt so uneasy, in fact, he couldn't even bring himself to look at her. Samia could sense something wasn't right. Finding the silence more awkward than conversation, no matter how forced, she continued to ask Paul questions—in French. Although she never dared bring up Vanessa.

"Why did you choose to live down here?" she asked, while flicking through her phone. "It's not the most obvious place to be."

"I'm not really sure," he answered, eyes fixed to the road. "I'd been down here before, when I was young, and I never really forgot it. I guess it put a spell on me."

"Do you find it tiring speaking French all the time? I can speak English if you'd prefer?" she offered.

"Yeah, I do, but equally tiring is listening to the French speak English," he laughed. "In fact it's much worse, but if you want to practice your English while we're together—I mean, while you're staying here—we can."

"I don't mind," she shrugged, "we can speak a mixed language, one only we can understand. Thanks again for having me, by the way."

"It's fine, it gets lonely in the villa anyhow," he replied, not glancing at her.

"I was just so miserable in Paris," she went on, "I needed to escape for a while."

"It's really fine," he repeated.

Sensing his unease she changed the subject. "Did you bring your cameras with you?"

"One or two," he replied.

"Could you teach me how to be a photographer," she asked.

"No," he shook his head, "I'd rather not. That's all behind me now," he muttered uneasily. "I don't take photos anymore. But if it's something you're interested in, of course I can help here and there."

"It's ok," she replied, "it's not important." She returned to her phone for the rest of the drive.

By the time they arrived at the villa, Paul felt exhausted. He wasn't sure if it was from the drive or from his anxiety around her. Samia, also unsure if the drive went well, if she'd made a good impression, if they were getting along or not, was glad when Paul suggested she explore the shore alone while he did some work. He showed her where the beach was and reassured her she'd be perfectly alone if she preferred to swim in the nude. He explained the route back to the town, about an hours walk depending on the sunlight, and told her the name of Denise's cafe in case she wanted to have a drink and meet some people. He pointed out the hills with the best views of the sea, so she could begin her photography career, and he offered her the use of his cameras. They arranged to meet back at the villa at three in the afternoon for a late lunch of rice and fish.

There was no work for Paul, of course there wasn't, there never was. But he just needed a moment to himself. A moment to work out what he was going to do with this young woman he'd invited into his life. Inside the villa he put a pot of coffee on the stove and watched Samia, who was overjoyed by the landscape she now found herself in, as she strolled down towards the sea, a red and white towel flung over her shoulder. Her walk suggested she was careless, free, at ease. Everything he wasn't.

He got up and tidied the bedroom, deciding it was best she had some privacy, then he prepared the couch as a bed for himself. He hauled her luggage, a suitcase about 3 feet tall, into the room. It weighed at least thirty kilos he guessed. What on earth had she brought? Did she plan on never leaving?

He heard the coffee bubbling on the stove and poured himself a cup. Then he sat at the desk which faced a window out to the sea and put his feet up. It was almost one in the afternoon, and the sun was high and ferocious.

Samia seemed nice, he thought, confident too. Much more confident than Vanessa had been the last time he'd seen her. Maybe it was a French thing? She'd saved the car trip from being a complete wreck, he was glad, and he had that to thank her for at least. Paul had surprised himself by how awkward he felt around her. Was it because she forced him to think of Vanessa? Her being there meant he could no longer ignore the fact he'd had a daughter once, and that his daughter had been stolen from him. She was gone for good.

Or was it that he found her beautiful? But why should that matter? She *was* beautiful, anyone would think so, there's nothing wrong with acknowledging that. Right?

Or was it because she looked Middle-Eastern? Because she was an Arab, or might be an Arab? And Paul had decided he didn't like Arabs anymore.

Did this actually bother him? Paul Greene, the man who once photographed refugees from Iraq as they crossed into Syria and froze to death in the mountains. The same man who took the jacket off his own back, in that bitingly cold valley in the Sinjar Mountains, and gave it to a dying man of about eighty, who prayed to Allah until his last breath was spent. He'd put his life on the line to tell their story, to open the world's eyes to their horror. The same man who once taught Waltzing Matilda to the Jordanian royal family while on a diplomatic mission for the Australian Government. The same man who publicly denounced the United States for invading Iraq, who lost his high profile job in New York because he was so outspoken against it. Who swore to never return to the United States while they occupied those ancient lands. Was that same man a racist?

No, he decided, no he wasn't. Of course he wasn't. So what if he felt uneasy around the Arab men at the train station, a man just like them had killed his daughter. The attacks in Paris were random, without warning, how could he be sure that those same men weren't plotting the next one, right there in Toulon. It was the only sensible way to be and Samia, seemingly a sensible person herself, would probably agree. Yes, sensible! But when had he started being sensible? Paul had never been sensible before.

Paul had been a swashbuckler, a rogue, a man who lived on the edge. He was ahead of his time, Raymond too. They all were, a whole generation of bad guys, too raw to tame and too handsome to shut down. But now the world had moved on and they were left behind, battered up in their shacks by the sea, as far away from meaningful society as possible, dreaming up ghost armies of terrorists to feel some semblance of relevance. They were desperate for a sign that yes, they did still matter, and no, their time wasn't over. But he knew it was a myth, a phantom, and here he sat now, concerned about being sensible. Sensible? What a horrid word, he thought.

Outside the window nothing was sensible. Was the sea sensible? Of course it wasn't, it was madness. What of the sun? A fiery mess ready to explode and engulf existence itself. And the hills? Nothing more than a surface for growing grapes, grapes to get man drunk, drunk enough to forget the mess of shit his life had become, drunk enough to pass out and hope he wouldn't have to wake up tomorrow. Is that sensible?

A drink, that's it, that's what he needed. Paul stood up and went to the kitchen and reached for a bottle of wine, he poured a glass and left the bottle out to breathe in case Samia would like some when she returned. But if she was an Arab, he wondered, and she probably was, she certainly looked that way, would she even drink? He hoped she would. The serenity of the sea was pointless without the dopey haze of drunkenness. The bountiful romanticism that sprung from fermented grapes was just about the only thing that kept him from drowning on those nights, those mad nights when the mad sea made the sensible man mad himself. Mad like he used to be, mad with love and hope and art and the cold whisper of death. When he used to be tenacious, when 'no' was just a word to scoff at. Now everything was 'no'. Now everything was sensible.

With the wine, Paul could sing and dance with Rebecca, he could admire Vanessa and kiss her on the cheek. He could hold them both, one in each arm, and talk about his plans for the future. Without the wine both Rebecca and Vanessa were very much dead, and he could only picture them dead or dying or sometimes begging to die. Rebecca in hospital, her head hairless, her gaunt face grey and twisted, her useless limbs flailing in the bed, desperate to get away, get away to anywhere that wasn't there. Desperate to just die.

And then Vanessa. Vanessa in how many pieces? None of them identifiable anymore. Mixed in with countless others, their flesh like offcuts on a butcher's tiles. No, he needed the wine, and he needed Samia to need the wine too, if she were to remain. He hoped she would, but was it just because she was beautiful?

He looked to the beach and saw she was returning. There was a cool breeze and she held the red and white towel around her tightly, her black hair was still wet and it barely moved in the wind. Her hips moved though, left to right and right to left, with each step.

It was almost three and he hadn't prepared the meal.

"Shit," he cursed himself as he rushed into the kitchen. He filled a pot with water and threw it on the stove. He went to the fridge and fished out the two fillets of herring he'd bought at the market a couple of days earlier. He tossed them onto a wooden chopping board and grabbed his carving knife as he heard Samia enter the villa.

"That water is amazing," she called from the other room. Paul put down the knife.

"It is, isn't it," he answered her, "I hope I never get too used to it."

"Surely," she said as she entered the kitchen, "if a man gets used to that, then the man is no longer living. Not in any meaningful way, at least."

"You sound like a philosopher," Paul joked.

"Well, I am French," she shrugged, "it is our national pastime, philosophising. How about Australians? What's your national pastime?"

"Drinking," Paul smiled, raising his wine glass, "what else? Care for one?"

"A swim in the sea followed by a glass of wine, you might have a hard time getting rid of me, Mr.Greene."

"Please, it's Paul."

Paul was relieved to find that she drank, and even more relieved that she did so enthusiastically. He showed her the bathroom and the bedroom, and after a short tug-o-war she agreed she'd sleep in it, with Paul on the couch. She had a hot shower and when she returned to the kitchen, wearing a white linen dress, Paul had the meal prepared on the table.

At first they ate in silence, which occasionally she broke to compliment the meal while he did so to offer her some more wine. Once lunch was over and Paul had cleared the plates, he suggested they drive into town to see if Raymond was at the bar and so she could acquaint herself with Denise. But Samia apologised for she was too tired, and needed a nap before dinner.

"That's fine," Paul said, "I'll call Raymond and tell him to meet us there after eight."

"Sounds lovely," Samia replied, "thanks again, Mr.Greene—sorry—Paul. It's very kind of you to let me stay here."

"My pleasure, Samia, it's kind of you to reach out. No one else ever did."

"We can talk about Vanessa tonight," she said, as she made her way into the bedroom. "Only if you're ready."

"I'd like that," Paul lied.

7

Raymond Bishop sat on his verandah and lit the bowl of his pipe. Below him he could hear the gentle whistling of the gardener as she trimmed at the sprawling hedges which flanked his driveway. What was that song she always whistled? he wondered. He'd heard it before somewhere, sometime long ago, when his bones didn't ache so damn much and his memory didn't fail him so constantly. When his blood pumped with gusto and his erection could last a whole evening. It was a nice song, a melancholic song, and he liked it very much. He liked to feel melancholic.

The day had been easy and relaxing, but now his body felt rotten, as it always did in the afternoon. He'd driven down to the sea and spent the morning snorkelling with his net around the shallows of Plage de Boukarou, searching for the dazzling lion-fish he'd seen there once. It had revealed itself two summers ago now, as it was lurking within the crevices of the rocks out beneath the point, where the waves charged like wild beasts and then collapsed like wounded ones. The fish was magnificent, with red and orange spikes like Roman spears and fins like shields. It had stared at him, looked into his eyes—his soul—and dared him to come closer, but he did not.

Back on shore no one had believed him when he'd told them he'd seen one. Lion fish weren't found in the Mediterranean, they laughed at him, but he knew what he'd seen and he was damn certain he'd see it again. Then he'd catch it and prove them all wrong. But today was not that day, he hadn't see it, and so he left the sea after an hour or two and ate an early lunch of salmon and fries at the cafeteria by the shore, while the legs of his table and chair were gently cleansed by the rising tide.

Now he sat alone on his verandah and ached. His left knee creaked in agony every time he'd shift it, while his right shoulder throbbed with a dull and dreary monotony he barely even noticed anymore. His neck, though, gave him the most grief. It'd grown stiff from too many years spent having to look over his shoulder, too many decades wasted glancing sideways at shadows. Now the nerve felt twisted, like a knot in a shoelace, and every time he looked around it tightened further. Raymond had made plenty of enemies in his life, it was how he knew his life had been well spent, and to the detriment of his neck he'd never stopped checking to see if they were right behind him. Good thing he did, though, as many times that was right where they had been.

"If people don't hate you for what you're doing then you're doing it wrong," he once told his biographer, a young journalist he'd met in a massage parlour in Crete. His biographer liked the line so much he used it for the title of Raymond's biography—*'Doing it Wrong'*. At first they'd both been proud of the book, but it hadn't sold like they'd expected it to, like they'd hoped, and the reviews were so damning it was considered a failure upon release. The young journalist swore to never write another book and quit the world of letters altogether. But to save his own pride, for pride was all he had left, Raymond anonymously (although it wasn't anonymous to anyone who knew him), bought six thousand copies, which were mostly still stored in the basement under his house. He had no idea what to do with them so he'd send them to friends for their birthdays, year after year after year. Paul had received no less than five.

The problem with the book, and Raymond knew it, was that it was only half true—if that. Little details got changed here and there to make it grander, bolder and easier to sell to the big Hollywood studios for the biopic he imagined selling out cinemas. An example being, and one picked up on quite quickly by the reviewer at the New York Times, was as innocent as his birthday. Raymond had been born on the 15th of June, 1936, not hard to discover for a seasoned journalist, but he made himself younger by a month and two days, writing his birthday as the 17th of July, 1936, the day on which civil war erupted in Spain. His father had been wounded fighting in Spain, the book explained—another embellishment—and Raymond felt there was a nice symmetry if he were born on the war's anniversary. A harmless enough fib, an innocent effort to connect with his father, and one he'd gotten away with—until it was picked up by that damned reviewer. From this grew forensic investigations from every other no-hope reviewer that followed. As it turned out, almost none of it held up. The book was almost entirely a farce.

What did hold up, though, were the chapters in Africa. All of that had been true, all of that had happened, and no one could take that away from him. Africa had conquered Raymond, civilised him, he'd like to say. He was the last of the old breed of colonialist who didn't look down on the tribal man as inferior, but as equal or greater than himself. He worshipped their men, admired their societies and devoured their women. No doubt he'd fathered a few children there on various assignments, but he could never be sure enough to bother finding out. That part was left out of the book.

"The curse of being good-looking and white in Africa," he'd once told a horrified diplomat in a bar in Nairobi, "is never getting the chance to meet your children."

But unlike Raymond, Africa had changed. It'd stopped being fun for him long ago. Disease had ravaged it, infighting had tainted it and the west had decimated it. The rest of the world looked on with scorn and pity, the same way they looked at Raymond after that damned biography had been published. The last time he'd spoken to the author he'd threatened him with lawsuits a mile long, the author in return had sued him for 'inconstancies of truth'. Raymond settled out of court and signed their last correspondence with that classic line, "If people don't hate you for what you're doing, then you're doing it wrong."

He looked at his watch, it was 5pm, time to get ready and go meet Paul at the cafe in town. Raymond was glad to have found Paul again, he really loved Paul when they'd been younger men. He saw elements of himself in the photographer who was twenty years his junior. Hell, all the rest of his friends had died long ago, Paul was all he had left. But Paul didn't seem the same to him, he seemed guarded, less frivolous than he'd been before. I guess that night with Rebecca still cut him deep, Raymond figured. Well, it shouldn't, if anyone ought to be mad it was Raymond himself, for wasn't it Paul who conveniently forgot to call Raymond when Rebecca had passed? Well, it wasn't worth dwelling on, was it? What was done was done, and if they were going to live so close to one another then the past was best left buried. Buried, just like Rebecca, that intelligent, tragic woman that Paul and Raymond had both loved so fiercely.

He got up from his chair and cleaned out his pipe in the living room, then he went down the stairs and spoke with the gardener for a brief moment.

"What's that damned song you keep whistling?" Raymond asked.

"I think, in English, it's called '*As Time Goes By*'," she answered.

He grunted something at her, then he put on his shoes and began the long walk towards the village. The sun still sat high, and it lit his beard with glints like silver flames. He whistled the tune the entire way.

8

Samia had slept well that afternoon. She found the cool breeze from the sea calming as she laid in the bed, drifting in and out of tender dreams. She'd sometimes raise herself on her elbows and peer out the window, at the maritime pine that tapped against the glass as the copper coloured finches bounced around its bough. There was nothing like that in Paris. What a wonderful idea, she thought, to come down here and be closer to nature. Time in nature is never wasted, Vanessa used to say, and Samia was beginning to understand what she'd meant.

At six in the evening, with the sun sitting low but deceptively hot, Paul knocked at her door to wake her.

"I thought we could head into town," he suggested, "there are some people I'd like you to meet."

"That sounds great," she replied, adjusting her hair in the mirror opposite the bed, "just give me a moment to find my shoes."

Samia was delighted by the drive to the village. As the sun faded away for the day there was a particularly dazzling sunset. Pink and yellow hues toyed with one another in the high branches of the oak trees.

"It's so lovely here," Samia said, "so much more beautiful than Paris."

"It certainly is," Paul agreed, as he did a hook-turn up a steep incline, "I dare say anywhere is more beautiful than Paris these days."

Samia threw him a look, "You are talking about my home, remember," she said, "Paris might have changed but it's still a magical city."

Paul kept his focus on the road. "When I was there, a few of months ago, I didn't see any magic," he said. "It was callous, cold, heartless. I've been to Paris so many times I wouldn't be able to remember them all, and it used to be special, I agree with you there, but now it is alien and hostile. Don't you think?"

Samia didn't say anything, she was a guest of Paul's and felt it best if she didn't rebut him too much, especially on their first day together. Instead she just looked at him, her expression blank. Paul seemed such a sad man, she thought, so wounded. She wanted to talk about Vanessa, and he did too, she could tell, but she didn't know the right way to go about it and nor did he. How could she tell him the truth, that Vanessa had meant everything to her, that she'd barely slept since that day, that she'd almost died herself, that she'd almost died many times since, by her own hand no less. How would she tell him any of that?

The car approached the village and Paul parked out the front of Denise's cafe.

"We're here," he said as he undid his seatbelt and climbed out of the car. "I'll show you around."

Denise was in a good mood that evening, for her and Achille had made love in the morning in his caravan down by the sea at Pamplonne. Achille, who was also at the bar, many drinks deep but showing no sign of drunkenness, was, despite his enormous size and brutish appearance, a very gentle and decent lover. He treated Denise as if she were a rare and delicate piece of coral, like the ones he collected along the sand outside his door. The ones he displayed proudly on the shelf just above his bed. Despite all this, however, Denise would not allow herself to get too close to Achille, not until he'd gotten his gambling under control. She hated to think how much of Paul's hundred thousand euros he must have already lost at the casinos in Saint-Tropez. Yet, at the same time, it made Achille tragic, and Denise, a devotee of romance fiction, loved nothing more than tragedy.

"Denise, Achille," Paul greeted them as he entered the bar and unwound his woollen scarf from his neck, "I want you to meet someone. Samia, this is Denise."

Samia was radiant, Denise thought, as radiant as the brilliant red of Raymond's Corvette, now shimmering in the dwindling sunlight outside the cafe. She hadn't seen a girl as beautiful as her in the village in many years, not since she was a young girl herself, surrounded by the more beautiful girls at her school, far more beautiful than Denise could dream of being. She rushed around to the other side of the bar to greet her.

"You are so lovely, my dear," she said as she kissed her on each cheek. "Tell me, how did you become the guest of a useless old fool like Paul?" she joked.

Samia looked to Paul, who seemingly only understood

half of what Denise had said, his French not bad but not fluent either. Unable to read him, she told a half-truth.

"I'm a friend of a friend, and I thought it might be nice to be out of Paris for a while. I just needed a sea-change."

"Well, let me give you my number, if you need any-thing at all, call me. Paul is not the best connected per-son in town, but I am."

Denise pulled up a stool for Samia by the bar as Paul sat next to her and ordered them both drinks. Samia liked the cafe, it was well-lit by large windows, and free of all the pretentiousness that the bars in Paris loved to flaunt. It was simple but cosy, basic but welcoming. The only thing she didn't like was the TV above the bathroom door. Samia found it hard to focus at times and the bright light of its screen tugged at her attention. Apart from Achille there were just two other men in the establishment, both of whom tried to steal a secret glance at the beauty, and both of whom were caught by Denise.

"This place is nice," Samia complimented Denise, "it's simple, but I like it."

Denise smiled, "Thank you, darling, with all the glitz and glamour of Saint-Tropez just up the road, it's im-portant to have something simple, something authentic, to balance it out."

Suddenly the bathroom door swung open and Ray-mond stumbled out, still doing up his fly. His presence was enormous, and the room suddenly felt crowded. Samia would never forget this first meeting.

"Imagine being a bullfighter, in a bullring in any old town in Spain," she'd tell a friend, many, many years later, "and then the gate opens and the bull enters the arena, and the bull is the most enormous, macho thing you've ever seen. And for whatever reason you're instantly attracted to it. That's how it felt when I met Raymond Bishop for the first time."

"No more *parlez vous-ing* that Gallic bullshit," Raymond bellowed, raising a finger to his lips, "this is a real bar, and in a real bar we speak a real language!"

"Scottish?" Paul asked, raising an eyebrow.

"Sure, why not! Let's call it Scottish. If anyone can understand half of what I'm saying then drinks are on me for the night!"

Achille, who spoke just a little English, and couldn't understand a word of whatever it was that Raymond spoke, picked up his glass and left the bar to sit at a table on his own, away from the obnoxious Scotsman. Denise was the only one who noticed.

"And to what do I owe this pleasure?" Raymond asked, taking Samia's hand in his own.

"Her name is Samia," Paul said, "a friend of a—"

Raymond raised his palm to block Paul's face. "Quiet now Paul, a young woman so majestic must surely have a voice of her own," he said.

"My name is Samia," she answered, Raymond finding her accent sweet and musical like the cooing of an exotic bird, "and you?"

"Raymond Bishop, the luckiest man alive, due to having just met you." He turned around to face his old friend. "Paul, we may need to do a re-write on that biography, I feel a chapter about to be written," he laughed. "Now tell me, young lady, are you in love with money?"

"It's a means to an end, so yes, why not?" she shrugged.

"Then I'd strongly advise you to marry me, for there's

no quicker way for a woman to become wealthy than marrying Raymond Bishop, and then divorcing quickly thereafter."

Samia laughed, as Raymond finally released her hand and turned his focus to Denise, desperate for a drink. Samia looked at the giant Scotsman and thought him quixotically alluring. His beard, a mix of black and grey with streaks of white, hid his true age and gave him an aura she couldn't quite understand. She looked to Paul, who was probably more handsome, she thought, but would look even better if he had a beard like Raymond's, rather than just the light stubble he wore. She was surprised that she found both the older men so attractive, and put it down to the fact that she'd never met men like them before. French men, she found, were standoffish, especially the older ones, where as these two had been so instantly warm.

As the evening wore on, Raymond held court over the group. He romanced Samia by telling her of Paul and his adventures through Africa, of wild nights hunting game in the Serengeti, of the million and one stars one could see while sleeping rough with the tribes of the Bedouin. Of the quiet stare of a buffalo in a drained marsh, the sun rising behind it.

"Times have changed, of course they have, and Africa too. Now it's just a scapegoat for the Nazi pundits on TV, who are overly eager to blame every shortcoming in the west on the brown and the black man. As if white man never did anything wrong?" Raymond lectured them.

"Oh come on," Paul repudiated him, "as much as I love the romance of Africa too, and the Middle-East, it can't be denied, Raymond, that their people are the ones waging war right now."

"I'd almost forgotten," Raymond turned to Paul, "what a racist bastard you'd become."

"That's bullshit," Paul defended himself, "I'm just saying it like it is, all those terrorist attacks across Europe these last few years, who's been responsible for them? They've been Syrian, Tunisian, Algerian, Iraqi. There's no denying facts, Raymond."

"You want a fact Paul? Seventy-five percent of terrorism on this continent is in Ireland by the Irish. Their skin is as white as their mother's milk!"

Paul went silent, he wasn't sure if what Raymond had said was true or not but he didn't want the conversation to continue, he could see that Samia was becoming uneasy, and he could feel an anger rising in his own chest.

"I'm sorry," Paul said to her, "you don't want to hear this."

"It's ok," Samia said, "you have suffered a lot at the hand of people from those places, but that doesn't mean you have to hate them all."

"Suffered!?" Raymond scoffed. "I'm sorry, love, not meaning to mock you, but please tell me in what way has this man suffered?"

"He lost his daughter, in the attacks in Paris, if that isn't suffering then what is?" she said.

Paul fell silent, as did Raymond. Samia looked between the two of them.

"You hadn't told him?" she asked Paul.

Paul shook his head.

"I'm so sorry," she said, "please, would you excuse me?"

Samia pushed past the men and went into the bathroom, Denise, who'd been eavesdropping on to the conversation, went to the door to hear if she was alright.

Raymond sat next to his old friend and put his arm around him.

"My god, man," Raymond said, "now I get it, everything makes sense."

"I should have told you earlier, it's just, I hadn't told anyone in such a long time and I'd forgotten how to."

"You were going to take it to the grave, weren't you?" Raymond asked.

"I was, yes, until she came along. They were friends, she emailed me and… "

"It's ok," Raymond reassured him, "you don't need to explain anything. When you want to talk, if you want to talk, you can. And if you don't? That's fine too. But one thing I will say, go easy on that Arab shit, the girl looks as if she may be one herself, it's not worth upsetting her for some bullshit you read online."

"Thanks Raymond," Paul said, gently removing Raymond's hand from his shoulder.

Samia came out of the bathroom, her eyes red.

"I think," she said, as she approached the two older men, "it's important this night isn't ruined, isn't ended like this. I have taken some time off my studies to enjoy myself, and as we are in a bar, I think we should forget this conversation and do a shot to celebrate my arrival."

"Three shots," Paul called to Denise, "no, make it four, pour yourself one. No, five, Achille you too," he shouted at the gambler, hunched over in the corner, lost in his fifteenth beer.

"One thing," Raymond interrupted the revelry, "before this gets too out of hand and we begin forgetting where the hell we are. What was your daughter's name, Paul?"

"Vanessa," Samia butted in, "her name was Vanessa, and she was the most incredible person to ever live."

9

A few days after the evening at the bar, Paul invited Samia to join him for a walk to the medieval hilltop town of Gassin. She climbed on the back of his motorbike and they rode as far as the village. Paul parked next to the pétanque courts, which were full of groups of elderly men and women partaking in a tournament. The sound of the pétanque balls knocking into one another, like the clack of oyster shells, reminded Samia of her childhood, when she'd play the game with her grandfather at the court in his village outside Algiers. Her grandfather was a wonderful player, and he'd only ever lost one game—to her grandmother on their first date. He'd always insisted he hadn't lost on purpose, but of course everyone knew it was a lie.

They climbed off the motorbike and walked away from the village, along a bike track that wound past small, sleepy factories before a calm and enchanting forest engulfed them. Samia always felt more at ease in nature, and her anxiety—which hung off her in the morning like unwanted company in a bar—began to loosen its grip. Paul's mood also steadily improved as they went further into the shade of the mighty oaks. He wasn't sure why he'd woken agitated, perhaps it was because he was having a tough time sleeping on the couch.

"So," Paul said, as he worked up the courage to breach the topic they'd both been ignoring, "how long did you know my daughter?"

Samia thought for a moment, had it been six or seven months? The first month they'd barely known one another at all, it wasn't until a party weeks into the semester when they'd finally taken the chance to have a proper conversation.

"Six months," she said, "maybe a little more."

"Was she happy in Paris?" Paul asked.

"Very happy, she loved it," Samia said, "she was so wrapt up in the architecture, the history. She'd spend every free day in one gallery or another. There are endless galleries in Paris, but I think Vanessa had visited them all at least twice. She said in Australia it is not like this, there is not so much culture or history."

"She was right," Paul said, "life in Australia is very good, very safe. But there's a sad kind of emptiness there which culture and art might normally fill. Also, the history is very tragic."

"Why is the history tragic? You know here in France the history is pretty bad."

"Yes I know, but Australia was a victim of the colonialists, the British especially, and a lot of people suffered for it. It creates an emptiness, a feeling of guilt, and no one is quite sure why they feel the way they do."

"It is very beautiful there, no?"

"It is beautiful, no doubt."

They passed through a clearing in the trees flanked by thawing vineyards void of grapes, and paused to pat some horses who were tied to stakes just off the track. Samia loved horses, probably more than anything else in the world, but she came from a poor family and she'd never had the chance to own one. As the forest began to trickle away they had their first glimpse of Gassin, humble and yet proud, high on the mountain like a crown on a prince.

"Raymond lives around here," Paul said as they started the ascent to the village.

"He's an interesting man," Samia commented, "I've never met anyone like him."

"He's definitely one a kind," Paul agreed. "Thank God. Men like Raymond don't last long in this world, but somehow he's kept on keeping on. He's like the Keith Richards of journalism."

"Who's Keith Richards?" Samia asked.

Paul looked at her, and he was reminded of the gap in their age for the first time. He had since he'd met her treated her as an equal, as being no different from himself, and Samia respected him for this and returned the gesture. But occasionally their 34 year age difference would show.

"He's a guitarist, the hardest living guitarist of all time, who's outliving all his peers with some kind of black magic."

"I bet you Raymond's into black magic," she mused.

"Quite likely," Paul agreed, "there's few things in life Raymond hasn't dabbled in."

"Was he into drugs?" she asked.

"Yes," Paul nodded, "we both were. I was probably

worse but he went pretty hard."

"What kind of drugs?" she continued.

"All of them," Paul shrugged.

"Even heroin?"

"For a while, yes. Why do you ask?"

"No reason."

"How about you, then?" he turned the conversation to her.

"Oh, you know," she looked down at the stream below her feet, "just the usual stuff. Vanessa never touched them though, not when I was around anyway."

"Why do I get the feeling you're lying to me?" he probed.

"Because I am," she smiled. "We should visit him," she suggested, as Paul led her further up the hill.

"Who?" he asked.

"Raymond, obviously."

"Sure," he said, "I'll give him a call when we're at the top."

Gassin was a beautiful town. Not as grand as some of its neighbours, but what it lacked in size it made up for in charm, and charmed Samia was. She'd brought a polaroid camera she'd purchased in Paris and photographed the doors, the small medieval details cemented along the stone walls and the strange little dogs with their incessant yapping. Paul showed her how to perfectly capture the light down the delicate, winding streets, which were partially obscured by the shade of enormous plane trees. He led her to the view over the landscape below, a patchwork of chateaus and estates which dwindled in size until it reached Saint-Tropez, glittering like a star as it nestled into its brilliant bay.

"Saint-Tropez looks beautiful," she said, as they sat on a ledge and unwrapped some sandwiches Paul had prepared that morning.

"I've never been," Paul admitted, "but something tells me I wouldn't like it."

"Well we have to go," she said, "it's very famous here in France, it would be silly to miss it."

"The way Raymond talks about it, Denise too, it sounds… toxic."

"You talk just like Vanessa," Samia smiled. "Well I want to go, even if it's on my own."

Paul went quiet and they ate.

After the sandwiches they shared a bottle of wine and feeling slightly drunk they laid down in the plaza in front of the sixteenth-century church. As Samia slept, Paul stayed mostly awake, enjoying the sunshine streaked across his face and the gentle hum of cicadas from the forest below. At one point Samia adjusted her position and two of her fingers came to rest in the palm of Paul's hand. He felt his heart begin to race. Had she done that on purpose?

Samia had proved to be a beguiling guest. On occasions when they'd spend time together, like the walk to Gassin, she'd open up and talk freely with Paul, sometimes even leading the conversation if he himself felt guarded. Other times, though, she'd sit alone and quiet, either by the poplar trees at the cliff face or down on the beach, and say nothing to Paul for entire mornings or afternoons. She'd just sit there and think, sit there and remember Vanessa, he assumed.

This didn't bother Paul, though, for he was glad his guest required little entertaining, but it meant there was something uncertain about the two of them together, something missing in their relationship. As her fingers laid delicately in the palm of his hand, he wondered what that could be.

After an hour or so of laying in the sun, Paul's alarm went off and they both got up.

"That was like a dream," Samia said, her eyes still dappled with sleep, while her jet-black hair reflected streaks of blue in the dopey haze of the setting sun.

Paul unlocked his phone and called Raymond, and after a brief conversation they agreed to meet at his house for the afternoon's drinks. He helped Samia to her feet, and they began the short walk to Raymond's.

The morning, weeks earlier, that Paul had awoken in Raymond's living room had been such a blur to him, that he hadn't quite appreciated the scale of his friend's home. A large wooden gate opened on to an impossibly long, stoney driveway with a fountain at the far end. The driveway was flanked by an army of enormous Moroccan palms which tilted in the afternoon breeze. The house itself was impressive, rising from the earth as if made from the very stone it stood on, surrounded by a dense jungle which Raymond had spent a quarter of his life cultivating. He had created his own oasis in the image of his fading memories of Africa, his memories of youth and vitality which had long passed him by.

As they approached the house he came out to greet his friends.

"My God," he said, brushing past Paul and hugging Samia, "I've had Bardot, Deneuve, Binoche and Birkin here at different stages of my life, for different reasons too I ought to add, but none of them looked half as beautiful as you do right now, standing in front of that fountain."

Samia laughed and hugged him back.

"Paul," Raymond called to his old friend, "make yourself useful and take our photo, weren't you on Magnum's books once?"

"But Paul doesn't take photos anymore," Samia teased, "I had to beg him to teach me just now in Gassin."

"When did you get so goddamn boring, Paul?" Raymond remonstrated his friend.

Paul noticed the camaraderie between Raymond and Samia and he felt an unexpected pang of jealousy, but he did his best to ignore it and took out Samia's camera. He took a photo of the two of them, smiling in the reflected light of the fountain, the Moroccan palms on guard just behind them, their arms around one another. He waited for the photo to print and handed it to her. It would be one of Samia's most treasured possessions for the rest of her life.

"How about a drink on the balcony?" Raymond suggested. "I've just finished preparing margaritas."

"That's the best idea I've heard all day," Samia beamed, "this one has had me hiking mountains in the blistering sun. It's not good for a girl's complexion," she joked as she winked at Paul.

Up on the balcony, with its view to the sea and the horizon, Raymond gave them each a drink and pointed out the landmarks.

"It's the sunset, though," he told them, his eyes glistening over a little, "the sunset which makes getting up every day worthwhile. You know, Samia, Paul and I aren't unlike that sunset. Once we were vibrant, blistering men, sailing high above the world and looking down on all the numpties, untouchable to anyone but the gods. You couldn't look at us for longer than a few seconds without burning your retinas. Then time happened and we started to slip a little, and we kept on slipping until we ended up like that ball of light on that damned horizon there, almost out of view, a mere shimmer of its former glory."

Samia turned to him with a reassuring look. "You're right, it is fading," she said, "but surely it is the most beautiful, right now, that is has been all day. Besides, it is still here for a while longer, no?"

"It's beautiful, sure, but beauty ain't worth nothing in this life, as you'll likely find out," Raymond sighed.

As the evening grew dark they moved inside where Samia was shocked to see a rhino's head on the wall, amongst the numerous other trophies.

"Are you a hunter, Raymond?" she asked her host.

"I was once, a long time ago, and I'll be honest with you I regret it, those wild ones anyway. But I do still enjoy hunting for boars now and then."

"My father hunts boars in the forests outside Paris, he calls it pest control."

"Well he's not wrong," Raymond scratched at his beard, "they are pests, especially down here, but they give a good fight and they don't die for nothing. The meat of a healthy boar will feed a village for a week. I do feel rotten about that rhino though, I leave it up there to remind myself of what a bastard I once was."

"You mean, what a bastard you still are," Paul chided him.

Raymond laughed, "You're not wrong, Mr.Greene,

they reserve a special place in hell for the likes of me."

"You should teach me to hunt," Samia interrupted them. "So long as it is eaten after, and the animal doesn't suffer unnecessarily, I can't see the harm."

Raymond looked at Paul, and then back at Samia with admiration in his eyes.

"What day is it?" he asked her.

"It's Tuesday, I think?" she replied.

"Perfect, Wednesday is a legal shooting day. I'll tell you what, why don't I put the two of you up here for the evening, you'll have a brilliant night's sleep, and then to-morrow, bright and early, we can jump in the truck and head out to the hills below Ramateulle. This time of year they'll be teaming with game, and I'll teach you how to shoot straight."

"I don't know, Raymond," Paul shifted uneasily on the couch, "I don't know if giving the girl a gun is the safest thing to do."

"The only thing unsafe would be giving you one, Paul. Let the girl decide what she wants to do."

"The girl has a name, gentlemen," Samia reproached them both, "and she'd love to go shooting tomorrow, so long as the conditions are good and the fight is fair."

"I feel for the beast that stumbles into your aim," Raymond laughed, admiring the young woman.

For the rest of the night they continued to drink steadily until Paul retired first. He laid down to sleep with a dull ache of jealousy bubbling in his gut, a jealousy he couldn't quite understand. A jealousy which kept him awake. Eventually he fell asleep just before dawn, and then Raymond rapped at the door just thirty minutes later.

"Get up, you bum!" he shouted from the other side. "It's time to shoot."

10

Raymond owned two single-shot rifles he'd had custom-made by a master craftsman in Bordeaux, a craftsman famed for producing the most beautiful rifles in all of France, if not Europe. He organised green and brown camouflage outfits for Paul and Samia, which fit them both surprisingly well, while he himself dressed in all khaki and donned a white pith helmet he'd been gifted from an Italian war general, a relic from the North Africa campaign of 1942—or so he'd been told. The helmet only came out for special occasions, he explained, and Paul thought he looked as if he were the antagonist in a low budget adaptation of a Joseph Conrad novel.

The drive to Ramateulle, which wound through a valley of oak trees and olive groves, didn't take them longer than fifteen minutes. When they approached the ancient walls Raymond turned to the right and found a parking spot in a convenient place outside the town. They briefly searched for a cafe but, as Raymond had expected, they were much too early.

"We'll survive," he said, "there's plenty to eat in the

backpack, enough to keep us in the fight at least. Now, does everyone have water?" he asked them.

Samia nodded as Paul complained about the lack of coffee, for he felt as if he were still mostly asleep.

"You'll just have to be a man today, Paul. I know that won't be easy for you, but let's get started and see how you do."

Raymond took the lead as they walked away from the town and down into the forest. Paul thought the landscape was more reminiscent of the Australian bush, with rocky crags and low lying shrubs, rather than the high, moist forests typical of this region. As they walked, Paul's frustration began to grow, and he began to remember why it was he hadn't tried to connect with Raymond for however many years it had been.

When they were younger men, Paul could match Raymond's vitality and wit, sometimes even beat it, but life had taken a toll on Paul in a way it hadn't on Raymond. Paul had suffered, real suffering, real loss. Paul had lost a wife and then a daughter, and Raymond's *c'est la vie* attitude didn't fly with Paul, it didn't resonate like it seemed to with Samia. It didn't excite him the same way it excited her. Paul had read Raymond's biography when it was released, and even though it made him pity Raymond, for the exaggerations were both plentiful and comical, he could see the sweetness in the myth of Raymond Bishop. The myth had been so finely crafted by the man himself, that over the years even Raymond had begun to take those myths as facts.

But watching him now—trudging along a dirt track outside a nowhere village in France, trying to win the fancy of a significantly younger woman, with a rifle in one hand and a canteen in another, Paul couldn't help but feel sorry for him. He was dressed like a drunk at a Hemingway look-a-like contest, stopping every now and then to reach for the binoculars dangling from his neck. Binoculars which probably didn't even work. He looked like a pantomime, and somehow Paul had become his hapless sidekick. On top of that, Raymond had showed little sympathy for Paul having lost his daughter, and had never even apologised for his tryst with Rebecca so many years ago, apart from a few moments of drunken word vomit. Paul could feel himself becoming furious.

"Quiet!" Raymond stopped them with an open palm. "There's something rustling in the bush over there."

Samia looked to Raymond for guidance as he pointed towards a slight cleft in the rocks opposite the valley, and she got dizzy with anticipation as he crouched and cocked his rifle.

"What a joke," Paul whispered to himself, as he begrudgingly followed Raymond's orders and got to his knees.

Raymond let off a single shot, which was not as loud as Samia was hoping it to be, and then two unidentifiable birds flew from the spot Raymond had hit.

"Damn it!" he muttered as he got to his feet. "Just some lousy, goddamn pigeons."

Paul got to his feet too, and as he did so he felt his head begin to throb even more than it had earlier. He closed his eyes a moment, but it only got worse.

"Let's go further down," Raymond commanded, "there's the mother of all beasts in this valley, I spotted her last week on a walk. If I get but a glimpse of her the whole village will be feasting well tonight."

"I'm going to have to apologise," Paul cut Raymond off, "I'm in no state for this, I barely slept last night and my head is in a world of pain."

"No," Samia begged him, "please stay Paul, just drink some water and your head will get better in no time."

"No, I really must lay down, water might have worked when I was your age, but the only thing for me now is to sleep."

"Please, Paul," Samia insisted.

"Let him go, Samia," Raymond butted in, "it's no good having a man on your team who doesn't want to play. And if his head hurts like he says it does he won't be shooting straight anyhow."

"Cheers, Raymond," Paul said, as he turned to leave them, trying not to make eye contact with Samia, "just play safe now."

"How about you do us a favour Paul, and don't go wandering through any shrubs. Samia's new at this game and she's likely to mistake you for a boar."

"He is a bore," Samia sulked.

As Paul left the two of them and continued back the way he'd come, he could hear their laughter and couldn't help but feel as if he were missing out on something, missing out on a chance to cement a bond with Samia. But the truth was his head did hurt and Raymond had been getting on his nerves ever since that night they'd spent at the bar with the two women.

He made it back to the road and continued along a path that wound around an empty carpark, shrouded with shade, and ended in a peaceful, overgrown park. The day was still young, not yet nine in the morning, and the area was perfectly quiet. He found a patch of grass to lay down on, already dried from the warming sun, and managed at last to sleep.

As he slept he dreamt of his daughter, the two of them on a ferry on Sydney Harbour, it's their last day together before she moves to France. He is seated next to her, his hand on her knee, as the harbour swirls around them like paint being mixed on a palette, tilting and turning with the boat. He begins to ask her something when her face morphs into Samia's. Her auburn hair melts into black as her blue eyes bulge into larger, brown ones. The eyes look up to him with tears in them.

"What's wrong," his dream-self asks her.

"You're what's wrong," replies the girl. "You've always been what's wrong."

Suddenly they're not on a boat anymore, and he finds himself falling down in the water, drowning, grasping for her hand as she hovers above him in the air. As the hand stretches down towards him he reaches up to grab it, when suddenly a blow strikes his face, and another and another. Suddenly he woke up with a violent start.

Paul sat up, rubbing his jaw, it was wet and hurt to touch.

"What the hell?" he asked himself. "This day needs to end."

As he looked up he saw in front of him the giant shape of an animal, its hot breath burning his face like steam from an iron. His body recoiled. Paul was shocked to realise he wasn't dreaming anymore, and even more shocked to discover he couldn't move. Fear had frozen him to his spot, resting on an elbow and facing down a monster.

The boar was enormous, the size of Raymond's Corvette, if not bigger, and its eyes, bubbling with a red and yellow broth, stared fiercely into his own. Two, jagged, pointed tusks curved up from its grotesque lips and hugged the shaft of its snout. The stench, like a corpse left to rot in a creek, overwhelmed him as the beast began to thrust its head closer and closer to his own.

Paul propped himself up higher, and using his right leg he kicked himself back a foot from the animal, only to have it make up the distance with a thrust of its short, muscular hind legs. Paul was scared, more scared than he'd ever been before, and he reached next to him in vain for his backpack. He remembered there was a knife in there, and if he could get it before the beast lunged at him again he might stand a chance of surviving the encounter, although he knew for sure he'd end up wounded. The only solace, Paul thought, in his last moment of clarity, was if the thing killed him, if it gored him to death or trampled him underfoot, he may at least see his wife and daughter again.

The boar thrust its head at Paul's leg and flung him back another foot as he rolled over himself. The move had put Paul within reach of the bag, though, and as he reached inside he was relieved to find that the knife was still there, the handle facing up. He got a good grip on it as the animal threw the entire weight of its enormous body on top of him.

What happened next was impossible for Paul to follow, and he would never be able to remember it clearly. The boar's hoof struck him under his arm, an excruciating wound that almost put him out of the fight, just as he managed to thrust the hunting knife right between its pulsating rib-cage. For a moment Paul was optimistic he'd win the battle, as the boar squealed and roared away from him, but then a pain unlike anything he'd ever felt before struck him in the right leg, and Paul was certain he was done. But suddenly, the boar, wild-eyed with fury, turned from Paul and darted off into the overgrowth, four of its young following closely behind.

Paul screamed out in pain and reached for his thigh, then he brought his hands to his face and saw they were soaked in blood. As his consciousness began to fade he heard the rapid hurry of footsteps descend from the hill above him, and as he closed his eyes the last thing he heard was Samia's voice.

"Oh my god!" she screamed. "You've shot him! Raymond, quick, you've shot Paul!"

11

When Samia was a young girl, bright and innocent and unusually intelligent, her parents told her stories of the horrors of the war in Algeria. They told her about her uncle, Youcef, also unusually intelligent for his age, who was a masterful mandolin player and unbeatable at chess when he was just eleven years old. On his twelfth birthday, Youcef's mother (Samia's grandmother), was wounded when a mortar bomb was dropped on their neighbours house by a French aircraft. Youcef, despite his smarts, had not yet began his studies and therefore had no knowledge of how the human body worked, let alone first-aid. Being the only one at home with her when the bomb had fallen he hurried out into the street, begging for help, screaming for someone, for anyone, to come and save his beloved mother. But either no one heard him that morning or no one dared leave their house for fear of becoming a victim themselves.

Youcef, soaked in a desperate sweat, rushed back inside where his mother was bleeding to death on the floor. He inspected her injuries and found there were too many to identify. There were wounds on her legs, her arms, her waist, her face. There was a large gash in her abdomen, sliced open by shrapnel, and her organs were threatening to spill out onto the floor. Youcef ran into the kitchen and found a carving knife. He set to cutting up the living room curtains, which had been thrown across the room in the blast, curtains his mother had made herself, and started applying the strips of cotton to her as if they were bandages. He knew that if he could stop the bleeding, then maybe—just maybe—he could save her life. And he did stop the bleeding, but he did not save her, for as another blast was heard across the narrow street, his mother grasped her son's face in her hands, the son she'd loved so much and dedicated her life to educating and caring for and said:

"Youcef, my boy, please go forth, and save the people of your country."

And then her eyes rolled over and her breath went away, as her heart, as big as any heart in Algiers, exploded in her chest. Her body convulsed and her fingers tightened around her son's shoulders as her painted red nails drew blood from his skin. Her organs finally spilled into his lap and then she went limp.

Youcef took his mother's dying wish as a command from Allah himself, and for the remainder of the war he studied the art of first-aid and saved the lives of countless countrymen, too many to know, until he himself was caught in an electrified fence, fleeing the French army, and his own heart exploded from the voltage. He was barely fourteen.

Samia kept Youcef close in her heart, almost like a

personal saint, and she too decided she'd dedicate her life
to saving others and was now in her final year of a nurs-
ing diploma in Paris. As Paul laid there, covered in blood,
wounded by a bullet from Raymond's gun, she hoped her
training would serve her well. She needed it to.

"Paul," she cried, as she knelt beside him, "Paul, please
respond."

She moved her hands over his body, searching for
the bullet's entry point, but she could find only a scratch
across his right thigh. Raymond hurried down and
crouched beside her.

"Bloody hell," Raymond muttered, "look at all this
blood. Had he just remained still I could've got the
damned animal between the eyes. He'll bleed out if we
don't stop it somehow."

"I can look after him," Samia instructed, "I just need
you to get the truck and get back here as fast as you possibly can."

Raymond raced away from the scene, back up the hill
towards his vehicle, as Samia checked Paul's breathing
and pulse. She took off her camouflage jacket and her
singlet underneath, and using Paul's knife she cut the singlet into strips she could tie around his limbs to slow the
blood loss, just as Youcef had done for his mother. But
then she realised it wasn't his blood that soaked him. His
wound, while possibly infected, was only surface deep. It
was the blood of the mother boar.

Suddenly Paul came to. He shifted a little as he tried
to pull himself up onto an elbow. But it was too difficult
and he groaned with agony as he collapsed back into
the blood-damp earth.

"What the hell happened," he asked, teeth clenched.

"Raymond shot you," she told him, "but it was an accident, I think. I need you to relax though Paul, please just lie still."

"Is it bad?" he asked. "Has that fucker finally killed me?"

"No Paul, the bullet only grazed you."

"Why am I bleeding so damn much then?" he swore as he looked down at his torso.

"It must have been the boar, did you strike it?"

"I got it right in the heart, just as it was about rip me apart with its tusks." Paul groaned again as Samia lifted his head from the grass and raised it to her lap. She noticed a tear in his outfit above his right pectoral muscle. She cut away at his jacket and found a light wound with heavy bruising.

A moment later Raymond's vehicle pulled up beside them and Raymond jumped out.

"How's he looking?" he asked.

"He's ok, he'll be fine. Do me a favour though, lift him a little and just support him," she instructed the much older man, "I need to suspend his right arm in a sling."

"You're a doctor then?"

"I'm a nurse, I will be soon anyhow. Now please, just raise him."

Raymond lifted his friend as Samia, using a strip of cloth that was once her singlet, supported Paul's arm in a sling. She did it with expert skill, which wasn't lost on Raymond who watched on with admiration. Paul opened his eyes again, still dazed from the attack, when he noticed Raymond behind him.

"You bastard," Paul muttered, "you tried to kill me."

"Trust me, Paul, had I tried to kill you you'd be dead. I was aiming for the boar, if you hadn't moved I would've had it in a clean shot."

"If I hadn't moved it would've gored my face off," Paul countered.

"Will you two just shut-up," Samia pleaded. "I am trying to fix this situation and all you two can do is have petty arguments. If you can't help me, Raymond, then just leave."

"If I leave how the hell are you gonna get him back to the villa?" Raymond asked.

"The villa? He needs a hospital!" she snapped back.

"No," Paul whispered through the pain, "please, no hospital. They'll ask too many questions. You said it was just a skin wound, right?"

"It may be infected Paul," she warned him.

"Didn't you just say you were a nurse? Surely an infection is easy enough to control. I hate hospitals, just take me home."

"I have to agree," Raymond interfered, "if we take him to a hospital they'll get the police involved and there'll be a paper trail a mile long. Let's just ease him back to health together, keep it our little secret."

"You bastard," Paul groaned, "you just don't want anyone knowing what a lousy shot you are."

Samia and Raymond lifted Paul into the back of the truck, carefully laying him out between Raymond's barrels of spare fuel. Then Samia supported his head with some old clothes and climbed in beside him. Raymond took the drive carefully, slowing almost to a stop at the impossibly tight turns which punctuated their way, as Samia kept a tight grip of Paul's hand. As they approached the villa the pain began to ease a little, and Paul lifted himself up and peered out of the truck. The view of the sea momentarily lifted his spirits. Raymond pulled up to a stop and climbed out of the vehicle.

"Samia, you sure you've got this?" Raymond asked as he helped her down from the back.

"We'll be fine," she reassured him, "if we need anything I'll ride into town."

"I'd stick around," he professed, "but if that boar is out there wounded it could cause a lot of damage to the next person who encounters it, I'll need to track it down and finish it off."

"It must be in a lot of pain," Samia said. "I don't think I'd like to hunt again."

"It's a rotten sport," Raymond admitted, "a rotten sport for rotten men."

Samia and Raymond helped Paul into the shower where they washed him down and then dried him off. After Raymond left, Samia sat down to inspect Paul's wounds. She was relieved to discover the gash on his leg wouldn't require stitches, and it looked as if no clothing had got caught in it so infections were unlikely. But still she cleaned it with a saline solution and applied some gauze she'd found in Raymond's truck. She felt around under his right arm and, despite the swelling, it seemed to her as if nothing was broken.

"You'll be in good shape again soon, Paul," she reassured him.

"I haven't been in good shape for twenty years," he joked. "But thank you, you're a wonderful nurse."

"You think so?" she asked, earnestly.

"Absolutely, it would've been a horrid mess had it just

been Raymond and I. I'm lucky you're here with me."

That afternoon Paul fell asleep before the sun had set and Samia, not wanting to stray too far from him, sat in the kitchen and stared out to sea. She was pleased with herself, she felt as if she'd done a good job and helped to ease Paul's suffering. Maybe even saved his life. Her uncle Youcef would have been proud. Then she thought back to that day in Paris, the day when Vanessa had been taken from her, taken from Paul. She had tried to help that day too, rushing to one of the explosion sights, pushing past the police as she attempted to convince them to let her through to the victims.

"I'm a nurse," she screamed as they held her back. "Please, let me help!"

But they would not, and they threatened her with arrest if she tried to interfere with the crime scene again. A friend of hers eventually managed to pull her away, already inconsolable, and drove her back to her parent's apartment on the Left Bank. Her mother made her a stew and sat with her arm around her on the couch, unable to take their eyes away from the television, desperate for every little detail of what had happened. Any clue as to why their city, their beautiful Paris, innocent and sweet and barely even relevant anymore, had been so brutally defiled.

She kept checking her phone, Vanessa had still not replied. She tried calling again and it just rang out.

"It will be fine," her mother had tried to reassure her, "your darling Vanessa will be fine."

It would be two hours later that Samia would receive a text, explaining that her darling Vanessa was not fine at all, that her darling Vanessa was in fact dead.

Samia then collapsed on the kitchen floor, her eyes wide open, her lips shut tight. She didn't cry, she didn't even move. Her mother had called for a doctor, but every doctor in the city was helping the victims, and they had no time for cases like Samia's. Three weeks would pass before Samia would say another word.

Outside the villa it was dark, and Samia rose to brush her teeth. As she did so, she heard a soft weeping coming from the bedroom. She went to the door, which she'd left ajar, and could see Paul curled over, his hands up to his face, crying in the dark. Samia entered the room, lifted up the blanket and climbed into the bed next to him. She put an arm around him, and he began to cry deeper now. He gripped her hand. She didn't cry though, she hadn't cried since that day in Paris. She had forgotten how.

The lighthouse lit the room, and she closed her eyes to sleep.

12

The following afternoon, Samia was out tending to the garden. She was removing weeds with tiny yellow flowers as she saw Raymond's Corvette approaching the villa from the hill. Paul was inside, propped up in bed and feeling sorry for himself, as he dealt with the stinging pain under his arm. He was vacantly flicking through his phone when he too noticed Raymond approaching.

"Samia!" he shouted to the girl, who was just outside his window.

"Yes?" she responded.

"Come inside would you?" he asked.

Samia took off her gloves and kicked the dirt off her boots as she entered the villa. She went into the bedroom where Paul's attention was fixed to the driveway.

"Do me a favour, tell Raymond I'm asleep or something, I'm really not that keen to see that man right now," he instructed her.

"He probably just wants to apologise," she said, as she adjusted the sling she'd applied to him after his shower.

"I don't want his apology, I don't want anything from him but to be left alone."

"It was an accident, Paul."

"Please, Samia, just do as I ask."

Samia relented and went out to greet Raymond. He climbed out of his car slowly, lacking his usual vitality which Samia found so charming. For the first time since she'd met him, Samia saw Raymond for what he was—a very old man.

"Raymond, how are you today?" she asked, as she walked over and kissed him on each cheek.

"I've been better," he admitted, kneading his fist into his back as he straightened out his posture. "How's the old codger going? Did he make it through the night?"

"He did," Samia smiled, "but not quietly. He's much better this morning, though."

"Let's go see him then, I have a story for him," Raymond said as he began marching towards the villa.

"No," Samia appealed, "please don't disturb him. He's just fallen asleep again, and I'm worried if we wake him he'll be in a terrible mood for the rest of the day. You don't have to live with him, I do," she said, forcing a laugh.

Raymond paused a moment, he had seen the two of them in conversation through the window as he'd driven down the driveway, he knew the girl was lying but he wasn't up for a fight.

"Fine," he said, "let him sleep, it'll do him well. Just let him know I found the boar that trampled him, it was with four piglets. I had to finish her off, the poor thing had suffered badly, but I managed to catch three of its young. I've taken them back to my place if you'd like to meet them, I'm thinking of naming them after my ex-wives."

Samia tried to smile at his joke, but the story of the dead mother and the orphaned young only made her miserable. "I'll let him know, Raymond."

Raymond smiled and climbed back into his car, he looked at the bedroom window and could see Paul, peering past the curtains, watching him leave.

Samia returned to the house and relayed the story to Paul, who felt relieved that the animal was no longer in pain.

"It surely suffered too much," he mused.

Later that evening they had a nap together in the bed, and woke up in each other's arms in the dark. The occasional wash of the lighthouse the only thing illuminating them.

"Where exactly is the lighthouse?" Samia asked, mesmerised by its glow.

"It's out on the island, where else?" Paul replied, his eyes still closed.

"Which island is it?"

"It's named Île du Levant," he said, "it's very close."

"Have you been?"

"No, not yet, but I've wanted to."

"Can we visit?" she asked.

"There are two ferries a day, from Le Lavandou. We could get one later in the week, when I'm in a little less pain. Although I wouldn't be able to get us there on the bike until my shoulder toughens up."

"I can ride the bike," Samia offered, "I have one in Paris. You'd just have to do your best to hold on."

"It shouldn't be a problem. There is one thing though,"

he said, "which I think may be a deal breaker."

"What is that?" she asked him, still haunted by the light.

"It's a nudist island. No clothes. Maybe my sling would be allowed, but not much else."

"That's fine," she said, "I love to be nude."

"Ok," Paul smiled, "later in the week, then."

Three days later Paul woke up feeling good. They climbed on his bike, with Samia in control and Paul behind her, his strong arm tight around her waist, and they drove out to Le Lavandou. She rode the bike well, accounting for the larger weight behind her with ease, and Paul enjoyed being able to relax and look out at the sea, its vibrancy hypnotic under the ultramarine blue of the sky. As they descended the hill towards Le Lavandou he gripped her a little tighter, and wished the ride would carry on for days.

They waited just twenty minutes for the ferry, which was empty apart from the two of them, and Paul began to feel nervous about undressing in front of her. She'd already seen him naked, when she and Raymond had washed the blood off him in the shower and cleaned his wounds, and in the days following when he needed help getting dressed. He hadn't seen her naked, though, and this made him uncomfortable.

What if he couldn't look away? What if he got aroused? What if she got offended, or became afraid of him, or felt somehow that he'd lured her there for other reasons? Sinister reasons. Or, what if she got aroused? What if it was actually her who had led him there for sinister reasons? What if he was the victim? And what if none of that happened, would they both be disappointed? Disheartened? Offended? Is it what they actually wanted? For something to happen?

When the ferry arrived at the island they were asked by a woman at the information centre to undress. She offered them sunscreen and a bag for their items, but they'd come prepared and didn't need either. Paul looked around the tiny office.

"Is there somewhere to get changed?" he asked the lady, who was nude herself behind the counter.

"Why not get changed here?" she suggested. "Your friend seems to have no problem doing so."

Paul turned around and was startled to see Samia entirely naked.

"Come on Paul, what are you hiding?" she joked. "Don't you remember? I've already seen everything."

Paul undressed, slowly and awkwardly thanks to his injuries, removing his sling and keeping his arm tight to his chest, and then joined Samia out in the plaza where she was enjoying the soft breath of sunshine on her already toasted skin. Despite the heat of an early summer, the island appeared to be mostly empty, with just a few older couples passing by. Paul noticed that none of them could look away from Samia, and he began to feel defensive.

"The lady at the desk suggested a small beach, on the the other side of the island, completely secluded," Paul said, wanting to rescue her from the prying eyes

"Let's check it out," Samia shrugged. "I'd like to take a nap around two in the afternoon," she continued, "when the sun is its hottest, so let's hurry."

They walked south from the town of Héliopolis, where the ferry had dropped them, along a golden, rocky coast, dotted with cactuses, wild olive trees and rosemary bushes. Paul, still somewhat injured, lagged behind Samia, and watched her as she bounced along the rocks. The arch of her back glistened with sweat. Out of respect Paul tried not to look, but Samia would capture his attention as she'd point out a bird or a lizard or an oddly shaped cloud. And once she had his attention he'd find it almost impossible to look away.

Eventually they reached the beach and were relieved to find it empty. As Paul spread out the towels in the shade, Samia ran straight into the water and dived under. When she came up for air she flicked her hair back and turned to him, laughing. Her breasts were in full view now, and Paul was transfixed.

"I've never felt so alive," she called to him, her voice carrying her smile across the breeze.

For a moment, Paul was afraid. He remembered how he'd felt when she and Raymond had excluded him in their jokes, the jealousy which he couldn't identify then was becoming apparent to him now. He'd been sleeping next to her for days, ever since the doomed hunting trip, and even though he never behaved inappropriately, never did anything he believed he shouldn't, he would occasionally brush up against her skin and his mind would go places he tried to resist. He had to remind himself why she was here, how they knew one another. She was his daughter's best friend. His daughter who had been killed, his daughter who he'd tried so desperately hard to forget because remembering her made living too painful. He watched Samia splash in the sea, she called out to him again to join her, and so he did.

"Isn't it amazing," she said as she swam up beside

him. "Who could believe we have all this to ourselves."

Paul smiled, and Samia noticed he blushed a little.

"It is amazing, although it makes the gash on my leg sting like hell," he said.

"The salt will just be helping it heal," she reassured him. "If you like I can rub some lotion into it when we get out?" she offered.

"No," Paul declined, "no, that won't be necessary." He dived under the water and swam away from her, as far as he possibly could in just the one breath. When he surfaced he remained alone. Not daring to glance in her direction.

When he finally came out from the sea, he saw that Samia was sun-baking on the sand. He went over and sat beside her, but not so close as to cast a shadow across her chest. She sat up a little and looked at him, he looked very handsome in the sunlight, she thought, she could even see hints of Vanessa.

"You know," she said, taking her glasses off, "we never talk about your daughter, do we?"

Paul kept his eyes focused on the sparkling, blinding horizon, and said nothing.

"I understand if you don't want to," Samia retreated, "but if you ever change your mind, I'd like to."

Paul took in a deep breath and turned to the young woman next to him, her skin coated in a fine wash of sand.

"It's just too hard, don't you think? It's just too hard to even think about her, let alone talk about her."

"What if I talked, and you listened?" Samia suggested.

"We can try," Paul said, after a moment's hesitation.

"Well," Samia sat up and shifted closer to him, their

arms almost touching, "I met Vanessa at a party. It was a party to celebrate the first break of the semester, and already she was very popular at the college, she never had a problem making friends. I remember seeing her, her hair so luxurious and full, her eyes so vivid and alive, and I knew right away I needed to know her. Over the next few weeks we started to see more of each other. She helped with my English and I helped her with her French. She told me about you, about her mother who'd passed away so long ago, and I told her about my family, about the war in Algeria, about my parent's struggle moving to Paris so that I could grow up in a place they thought to be safe. We became very close, inseparable almost, and stopped going to parties altogether as we preferred to be alone, just the two of us. We'd talk about film and literature and we'd smoke cigarettes on her balcony. Did you know your daughter smoked?" she asked him.

He shook his head.

"Well, she did. And she drank too, a lot, even more than me and I love to drink. But she was never angry or sad or depressed when she drank, she was happy and alive and excited. I loved to drink with her."

"Her mother was exactly the same," Paul remembered, "a night out with her never ended badly."

"And our first kiss, Paul, it was magical, unlike any kiss I've ever known."

Samia went quiet, her eyes fixed to the sea, as Paul turned to face her. Neither of them said anything, as a cold chill suddenly blew across the sand and Samia hugged herself.

"You and Vanessa were together?" Paul asked.

Samia turned to him, her eyes slightly squinted, her mouth curled in a bemused grin.

"Wasn't that obvious Paul?" she asked. "I thought for sure that would have been obvious?"

"It wasn't," he replied sharply. "It wasn't at all."

Samia said nothing, and just stared at him, slightly embarrassed.

Paul turned away from her, then he got to his feet and collected his belongings. Without saying anything else he made his way back to the ferry wharf, leaving Samia behind. He felt a dry nauseousness rising in his gut, and he wasn't sure why.

13

For the rest of the afternoon Paul was in a terrible mood. He tried to hide it from Samia, he didn't want to talk about it because he himself didn't understand why he was so angry. On the ferry back to Le Lavandou the wind was fierce and Paul sat inside the cabin, while Samia, her hair blowing furiously behind her, sat out on the stern deck, alone. She sat with her arms crossed tight in front of her, and every time Paul dared to glance in her direction she threw him a disquieting look. The day had ended very badly.

When they arrived back at Le Lavandou, Samia stormed past Paul as he was about to disembark the ferry. He caught up to her and offered her the keys to his motorbike.

"No," she said, as she brushed him aside and headed towards the port town, "keep them. Ride home yourself."

"I can't!" Paul shouted behind her. "Have you forgotten about my arm?"

"Then walk!" she called out to him, not bothering to look back.

Paul decided it was best to just let her go, he knew he was likely to make things worse if he said anything. He'd upset her, somehow, probably by reacting the way he did when she'd revealed the truth about Vanessa. But that had upset him too, and were his feelings not worth acknowledging as well? Instead of chasing after her he found a bar protected from the wind and ordered a beer.

"How's your day been?" the bartender asked in English, having correctly assumed that Paul wasn't French.

"Fine," Paul replied, "I went out to the island."

"Ah, *tres bien*," the bartender responded, "the island is an enchanting place, they say that if a man visits it even just once, he can never be the same again."

"In a good way or a bad way?" Paul asked, taking a long and satisfying sip of beer.

"Well, that depends on the man, of course. Life is subjective, and if the man would like to be happy—he will be! And if he'd like to miserable? Well, he'll find that even easier."

"Why is every bartender in France a philosopher?" Paul asked.

"What you mean to ask," the man smiled, "is—why is every philosopher in France a bartender?"

By the time the sun had set, Paul was well on his way to drunkenness, and he decided he'd better find Samia or else he'd be paying a small fortune for a taxi back to the villa or for a room in the town. The only problem, Paul thought, is where the hell had she gone? Paul paid his tab and left the bartender a healthy tip before making his way out into the narrow streets that led away from the harbour and towards the charmless main road.

The town was quiet now, with just a few restaurants and bars open. None of them were particularly busy, though, as the orange street lamps sprung to life and the stars began to shimmer above the sea. He'd spent more than half an hour poking his head into every open doorway, his search becoming more desperate, before he finally found her. She was sitting at the bar of a dingy rock n' roll joint, with a half-empty bottle of wine beside her and barely illuminated by the light from her phone. In fact the whole place was mostly dark, apart from some fairy-lights around the bar and a few neon signs, flickering orange and blue. The music was blasting from crackling speakers in the corner of the room, playing some kind of French heavy-metal which made Paul anxious. Paul approached Samia and pulled up a stool.

"Didn't know you were into rock n' roll," he said, as he tried to catch the attention of the bartender.

"I'm not," Samia replied, "I just wanted to go somewhere you'd never find me."

"Well, you chose the right place, this was the last bar I checked. I almost gave up."

"Good, then leave."

"I don't want to, I want to talk to you."

She swung around to face Paul, a look of vindictiveness sewn to her face.

"You want to talk to me?" she fumed, banging her wine glass on the bar loud enough to distract the bartender away from his phone. "You didn't want to talk to me on the beach, did you? You didn't want to know about my relationship with your fucking daughter then, did you? You just left me there, cold and naked in the wind, completely alone. And then on the boat, worst of all, when I was fucking freezing you just ignored me the whole trip. You didn't want to talk to me then, but you want to talk to me now?"

"I'm sorry," Paul lamented, "I just didn't know what to say." He looked back to the bartender who was pretending not to eavesdrop and gestured towards the whiskey. The bartender obliged and poured a glass.

"So?" she asked. "Do you know what to say now? Or is this all a waste of my fucking time? Is this whole trip a waste of my fucking time?" She looked away, feeling as if she were about to cry, although she was relieved to remember that she no longer could.

Paul didn't know what to say, in fact his whole life he'd never really known what to say. He wanted to make the situation better, but he wasn't sure why it was so bad in the first place. So his daughter was a lesbian? What of it? Paul had had plenty of gay friends over the years, men and women, and he never thought anything of it. Their business was their business. Why did this bother him so much then? he wondered. Was it because he'd fallen in love?

"Samia, look," he pleaded, as she pretended to ignore him. "It's a lot for me to register right now."

"What is?" she asked, as she threw her attention back to him

"You know what."

"No, I don't, Paul. Please, spell it out," she demanded. "Spell it out for the poor little girl."

"It's a lot for me to find out that my daughter was gay, that she was in a relationship with you, with a woman, and that she never told me."

"And you are disgusted by it?"

"No, of course I'm not, not at all."

"Maybe she didn't tell you because she knew you would behave like this?"

"Behave like what?" Paul refuted. He was drunk now, drunk and tired of acting like he'd done something wrong. He knew he'd regret it later, but if she wanted to fight then he was willing to.

"Like a fucking bastard," she spat at him, before turning away again.

Paul drank what was left of his whiskey and stood up, he turned to the bartender and asked for the cheque.

"Four euros is cool," the bartender replied, before collecting the coins Paul slammed on the bar.

"You know, Samia," Paul returned his focus back to her, "I've been pretty good to you these last few weeks, I've been kind to you. I've fed you, introduced you to people. I've done my best to make things normal between us."

"Normal?" Samia repeated as she faced him.

"Yes, normal."

"Why shouldn't things be normal, Paul?"

"Because we're different, and it's hard, the whole situuation is hard."

"And why are we different?" she continued.

"We're different because we're different, that's why!"

"But why? What exactly makes us different?"

Paul turned to leave. "I've had enough of this, Samia, I'm going to find a hotel and you'd do well to do likewise."

Samia stood up and followed him to the doorway, feeling light on drunken legs as she leant against the high-top tables. Just as Paul was about to leave, she stopped him with a comment. A comment she'd immediately regret, a comment which was made even more regrettable by Paul's response.

"Is it because I'm an Arab, Paul? Is that why things are hard? Is that what makes us so different?"

For the rest of his life Paul would wish he'd chosen his next words differently. In fact, he'd wish he'd just said nothing at all. But he had. And he had to live with that.

"Well, Samia, it was a fucking Arab who killed her, wasn't it?"

14

Denise wished a good night to her final customer, and locked the glass sliding doors. She went behind the bar and poured herself a generous glass of vermouth and sat at a stool alone. It'd been a hard day's work, again, and she could feel it in her joints. They were throbbing now with the early agonies of arthritis. She kicked off her right shoe and twisted her foot up so it could rest on her thigh, then she took a swig of her drink and began massaging her ankle, gently at first then rigorously soon after.

Just a few years ago, Denise had still felt young. She'd had the vivaciousness to party until dawn and the guile to swim in the sea at midnight with lovers whose names she'd never bother asking. She'd go on hikes through mountain passes without telling anyone where she was heading, and then not return for days. She'd had the stamina to make love again and again and again. But the last few years had ruined Denise, and she wasn't entirely sure why. The decline into middle age had been both premature and accelerated, and the woman she was only half a decade earlier had all but vanished. The two things she'd kept though, were her humour and her compassion, and while the rest of her had faded, these two qualities had blossomed, and this made her a lucky woman, she forced herself to believe. Because if she didn't believe at least that, then she'd be miserable.

I have Achille, she thought, and he is a hopeless man who needs caring for. What a gift to care for a hopeless man, especially a man as hopeless as he. And now I have the girl, too, and what a beauty she is. She needs a special care, being so young and so easily hurt. I'll care for her good, like a mother would.

Three days earlier, Samia had turned up at Denise's cafe early in the morning, she was shivering in the cold and Denise brought her in and gave her a change of clothes and fed her some spaghetti.

"What's happened?" Denise asked.

"Paul is an asshole," Samia replied.

Denise guessed at what could have happened. Did the Australian make a pass at her? If he had, well, Denise wasn't surprised. The Australian did, after all, have the air of a rogue who would surely be at the mercy of this young woman's charms. Or did the girl make a pass at the Australian? And did he reject her? The Australian was a wounded man, quite likely too wounded for love, and the girl was very young and beautiful and she would not have accepted this. She would have demanded he submit to her.

"You can stay here for as long as you need," Denise promised her as she engulfed her in a hug. "And if you like, I can tell Paul to stay away while you are here."

"It's ok," Samia said, "I don't think Paul will be

showing his face for a while. He'd have some nerve if he did."

"Then there won't be any problems," Denise reassured her.

There was nothing in the world that made Denise quite so content as having a desperate soul to care for, and now she had two. Had she been able to have children, she wondered, would her life have been any different? Would she still work in a bar? Would she still finish her shifts after midnight, and then begin again the next morning before dawn? Oh well, it didn't matter, her cards had been dealt and Denise had made peace with the fact she would likely die behind the bar, almost certainly alone too, as nothing was surer than Achille dying before her, probably of suicide, she figured. Gamblers always die of suicide, even if they win more often than they lose, their whole life is one long suicide and Achille's wasn't far off. Oh well, Denise shrugged, at least she'd have him for a few more years, hopefully, and Achille's suicide would be something romantic, after all, for he was very well read. She just hoped the girl wouldn't suicide.

Denise put her shoe back on, her ankle somewhat more comfortable from the massage, and turned off the lights in the bar. Then she went upstairs and stopped outside Samia's room and listened, she could hear sobbing, but not crying. Crying sounded different.

She knocked on the door, softly enough not to startle her, and bent down to the keyhole.

"It's Denise," she whispered.

"Come in," she heard Samia say, "it's unlocked."

Denise closed the door behind her and sat at the

end of her bed, she rubbed the girl's thigh as the gentle moonlight streaked across her waist.

"Can you stay with me?" Samia asked.

"Of course," Denise assured her, as she took off her shoes again and laid next to her. "Forget about him, don't waste your energy."

"Him?" Samia asked. "I'm not crying for him, I'm crying for her."

Denise kissed her hair, and she felt as if she were the luckiest woman alive. Soon Samia fell asleep, and eventually Denise did too, despite her ankles once again throbbing with pain. The lighthouse, so overwhelming in the villa, barely made a mark.

While Samia stayed above the cafe with Denise, Paul was at the villa alone. He was miserable. The morning after their argument at Le Lavandou he woke up in a cheap motel just off the highway. His phone had no battery and he had no idea where Samia might have gone. He was relieved to discover the keys to his motorbike in his pocket and he rode with some difficulty into the village to search for her. The first place he stopped was the cafe and Denise explained to him Samia had arrived a few hours earlier, and that it was for the best if Paul stayed away for a while. Denise would take care of her, she reassured him. Paul agreed and rode back to the villa, where he parked his bike in the dirt and went inside. He'd come so accustomed to having Samia around that the place now felt desolate. He decided the only thing to do was to to drink.

Without her, Paul no longer liked the villa. The sea, which had been so pleasant to look upon with her, to sit beside, had become callous and grey again. The garden, which she'd worked on tirelessly while he'd prepare her lunch, looked ugly and unkept once more. The bed which they'd shared, shared innocently and decently, shared in the memory and the pain of their lost Vanessa, was no longer desirable, and so Paul slept on the couch once more.

In one way or another Paul had come to love the girl, and now she hated him and hated him with good reason. If Vanessa were still alive she would have hated him too, he figured, and then she would have run off with her lover to be as far away from him as possible. But then again if Vanessa were still alive, he never would have said that about Arabs, he never would have hated them to start with. But she wasn't alive and he did hate them, he hated them for taking her and now having taken Samia too. He hated them more than ever. But he hated himself the most.

A week or so later it stormed. It was a dry storm with little to no rainfall. It was the kind of storm which Raymond had warned was common in these parts, with sickening cracks of lightning playing chase along the disappeared horizon. Paul, well on his way to drunkenness, braved the outside as the wind wrestled him to the earth. He battled on as far as his reliable poplar tree, it's own self bent to the earth after countless, similar battles, and he gripped it tightly. Then he began to shout against the gale.

He looked to the cliff, it's sharp edge beckoning him closer, and he decided he'd jump. He went to scream, like he did on nights like these, but he couldn't, there were no screams left. All the rage and fury had been whittled away to something less urgent, something pathetic. He knew the end was now. Without Rebecca he would be forever alone, and without Vanessa his heart was full of hate. And without Samia, well he never had Samia, but he felt even more empty for her absence all the same. He released his grip on the brave old tree and walked towards the edge of the cliff face, the whole time battling to remain upright against the violent winds. Approaching the edge he could see the rocks below through the thrashing of the whitewash, and then he looked towards the lighthouse. He couldn't see it, the clouds had shrouded it so completely that its light could not break through.

"Oh well," he thought, "what of it? That damn lighthouse has caused me nothing but trouble anyway, I'm glad to never have to see it again."

But then the clouds did break, just a little, and the light hit him. It hit his face, and it lit up the villa, the villa he had shared with Samia. It lit up the garden, the vineyards on the hill, the beach which he'd come to love. It lit up something in his heart, and he wondered—was this really the end?

Then, like the charge of an elephant, the wind belted Paul back to the earth, back away from the cliff, and sent him rolling in the mud. He began to crawl towards the tree when he was lifted up again and thrown against the trunk. He crawled under its branches and gripped on as tightly as he could manage, as all manner of shrapnel from the garden flew over the top of him and dug their sharp edges into the earth. He gripped on for his life, his life he now suddenly held dear, his life he was willing to forsake just moments ago.

"If I die tonight, then," he said to himself through

gritted teeth, "at least it won't be by my own hand."

But Paul didn't die, and in the morning when he woke up, the storm having passed, covered in mud and hidden under the poplar tree, Paul knew what he had to do. He had to see Samia. And he had to see her immediately.

15

Since Denise had been so kind to Samia, Samia had the urge to return the kindness. One morning she woke up to find Denise rushing around the cafe more stressed than usual, and saw an opportunity.

"Are you ok?" she asked, as she took a place at the bar while Denise prepared her a coffee.

"I'm not, no. Not at all. Achille was last seen entering the casino at Cavaliaire two days ago, and has not been heard of since. I can't imagine where he is."

"Then you must go search for him," Samia told her.

"How can I?" Denise shrugged her shoulders. "There is no-one who can help me in this cafe, and if I close the cafe for even just a day, I'll fall behind in my expenses. It's a cursed life I lead."

"I can run the cafe for you," Samia offered. "I've worked in bars in Paris. I can make coffees, I can pour beers."

Denise paused a moment and stared at the girl. Now she understood everything, everything made sense. Why the girl had arrived, why Denise had taken care of her, why Paul had betrayed her and caused the girl to seek Denise out. It was all leading up to this exact moment, when Achille needed her most, when he was either dead or dying and she couldn't be there with him, that the girl would come in useful. It was like something out of a book, she thought.

"My love," Denise stroked her face, "if you could do this for me I would be forever in your debt."

"Nonsense," Samia laughed, "it is I who owe you everything. This last week you have cared for me like your own child."

"Ha, you are joking my dear. Look at me, and look at Achille, now imagine we could have a child, which we can't. That child, probably a daughter, would not have just one percent of your beauty and charm. If she were to work for me I'd have her in the kitchen where she couldn't be seen."

Samia laughed. "That is very harsh Denise. You do know, beauty is only skin deep, right?"

"That may be so but that doesn't mean it should be discounted. Take this landscape here, with the vineyards and the pink sunsets and the chateaus out of story-books and the endless back and forth of the sea. You take away all those things and what do you have? You take away all that beauty and you're left with just the drunks and the gamblers and the whores. The beauty binds them together, and somehow the place becomes magical, just like you."

"I'm afraid you think too much of me," Samia blushed.

"And I'm afraid you think too little of yourself," Denise countered her. "Now, let me show you how to run this dump."

Denise went over all the basics of looking after the cafe—how to work the till, how to explain the menu, how to pour the perfect glass of wine—and then she walked to the bus stop to catch the next bus to Cavaliaire. Her plan of attack was simple, check the casino first, then the bars, then the bottoms of the cliffs. Had Achille actually done it this time she'd be proud of his courage, for it can't be easy, but she knew she'd miss him at the same time. Either way, she figured, the day would have an ending worth talking about back at the cafe.

Samia was at ease behind the bar, and she was surprised to find it busier than she'd ever seen it before. There were countless men coming in for coffees who'd never once visited in the past, and even a few women. She was taken aback when she realised that none of them could take their eyes off her. If she caught them staring they'd glance away for a moment before stealing another look. The customers in Paris weren't quite so needy, she recalled. But here in the cafe at least they were all polite, and had no problem waiting an extra fifteen minutes while Samia did her best to balance all their orders. On top of this they all left generous tips. She had some help from the chef, Pierre, but Pierre was a quiet man who preferred to be alone in the kitchen as much as he possibly could, and he was so fat that Samia found it impossible to move around him when he came into the bar, so she preferred to move slowly but alone.

As the lunch rush died away she found fifteen minutes to take a break, so she poured herself a glass of wine and lit a cigarette and sat in the gutter outside. She'd enjoyed her day, and hoped Denise would be willing to let her do more shifts in the future, even if she didn't pay her she was happy to help out. As she put out her cigarette, she turned to go back inside when she heard the familiar rumble of Paul's motorbike. It was a sound she recognised instantly, as it was exactly the same sound her own motorbike made back in Paris. It was her favourite sound in the world.

As Paul parked the bike opposite the cafe, she finished off her wine and hurried back inside. She went into the bathroom and arranged her hair, making sure she looked ok, although she wasn't sure why she cared. As she exited, she found Paul waiting at the bar, he looked terrible. She walked over coolly, calmly.

"I'm sorry sir," she said, her eyes lowered, "but unfortunately I won't be able to help you today."

"Samia," Paul pleaded, "I just want to—"

"What?" she cut him off. "You just want to what, Paul? You just want to have a coffee? A beer? Well I'm afraid that will be impossible as Denise isn't here today, only me, and as you may or may not have noticed I'm an Arab, Paul, and we both know too well how you feel about Arabs, so there'll be no one to serve you."

"I'm sorry," Paul professed. "To be honest I can't even remember what I said, but I know it was wrong, I know it was hateful, and I didn't mean it."

"Yes you did," Samia snapped at him, attracting the attention of Pierre who was sharpening knives over in the kitchen. He waved a knife at her, to see if she wanted some back up, but she shook her head. "Of course you meant what you said Paul, because it's true, it was an Arab that killed her. But instead of thinking like a logical man, and realising that one bad Arab does not mean the whole Arab world is evil, you choose to hate. So don't tell me you didn't mean it Paul, because you did."

"Alright, I did!" he professed. "What if I did? It's not like I want things to be this way, I don't want to think this way, but I'm not sure what else to do." He collapsed now, into a stool at the bar, his head in his hands. All at once Samia felt sorry for him, but then she replayed his comment in her mind and dismissed her pity.

"You need to change the way you think, Paul, because the way you think now is rotten."

"Then teach me," he begged.

"Teach you what? How old are you, Paul? A hundred? And you still don't know that blaming an entire race for the actions of a few is stupid? If you don't know this at your age then I don't think you ever will."

Paul lifted his head a little and looked at her, she was staring fiercely into his eyes, her own eyes red and watery as she fought back tears. Was she really about to cry now, over this, when she hadn't once cried for Vanessa? Paul sat up and reached for his keys, he collected them and swung off the stool. At the door he turned to her and smiled.

Later that evening Denise returned to the cafe, alone. Samia was behind the bar, carefully balancing coasters to make a small tower, doing whatever she could to keep her mind distracted. There were only two customers now, engaged in an animated conversation about a football match at a table in the corner. It had been so quiet that evening Pierre had gone home an hour earlier.

"How did you go?" Denise asked as she startled the girl, causing her tower to collapse.

"Oh, fine," Samia said, straightening out her apron. "The day was very busy, but the night was very quiet. I enjoyed myself though, mostly. How did you go?"

"I found him, in one piece, just. He is back in his caravan by the sea, cursing himself for his sins. The good news is he won't be gambling, for a while at least, as he has nothing left to lose."

"Oh, I'm so sorry, Denise," Samia said.

"Don't be. When the gambler has nothing left he stops being a gambler and starts becoming a man, and when Achille is a man I can feel like a woman again."

"But you are a woman Denise, a wonderful woman," Samia went around to the other side of the bar and hugged her.

"You can finish up my dear, I'll close it all down."

"Ok," Samia said as she untied her apron, then she asked, "Denise, can you call a taxi for me?"

"Where are you going?"

"To the villa, I need to apologise to Paul."

"I thought he was the one who needed to apologise?"

"He was, and then he did, but I said something I shouldn't have."

"I'll order one now."

The evening was calm and still. The violence of the storm had scattered debris all over the roads and toppled a few trees, but apart from that one would never have known there'd been anything other than peace.

When Samia arrived at the villa she thanked the driver and knocked at the door. When there was no answer she turned the knob and went inside.

"Paul?" she called from the kitchen, but there was no response. She looked in the bedroom, then the living room and was disheartened by the mess. There were items and pieces of clothing strewn around the place, as well as empty pizza boxes, cigarette butts and an unknowable amount of wine bottles. He's gone insane, she thought.

Suddenly she heard a creak behind her and swung around to find Paul standing there, brandishing one of the wine bottles above his head. Samia shrieked.

"What the hell?" Paul said as he lowered the bottle, "I thought you were an intruder. I was ready to murder you."

"No, Paul, just me," she responded, still guarding her head with her hands.

"You scared the hell out of me."

"I'm sorry, Paul."

"Don't be, I'm glad you're here. Want a drink?" he asked as he went to the kitchen, still shaking from the fright.

"No, I'm sorry for saying you were a hundred years old, that was cruel of me."

"Oh, forget about it, I've been called plenty of things worse than old in my time. Besides I am old, look at me, what other word could you use?"

"But you're not Paul, your energy is young."

"Young enough to still be racist? I don't think so. Racism is an old man's disease and I'm afraid I've caught it."

"It can be cured though, it's like anything else," Samia assured him, as she poured herself a wine and sat at the kitchen table.

"Bullshit, it's like cancer, once you've got it it grows and grows inside you until it shuts you down completely. It's best you just leave me here, Samia, return to Paris and forget about me. God knows the rest of the world has," he said as he joined her at the table, shifting a bunch of empty bottles to make way for his elbows.

"Paul, I have an idea," she said. "If you want to apologise to me, and mean it, then I need to see it in your actions, and not just your words."

"Forget it, Samia."

"Please Paul," she insisted, "just listen. Now, you have an issue with Arabic people because the attackers in Paris who killed your daughter were Arabic, and maybe you haven't known any Arabs before."

"I've known plenty," Paul said, "good ones too, some I even loved. But things change. Things happen and then one day you look in the mirror and you don't even recognise the person staring back."

"Exactly, things change. Like when you met me. And I know you care for me Paul because I see it in your eyes, I saw it on the beach before you were so cruel to me."

"I've said sorry," he interrupted.

"I know. But now you think that maybe I am the exception, not the rule, and I have an idea to teach you otherwise."

"I'm listening."

"Good. Now, look around this place, look around this

villa," Samia said as she stood up and gestured for Paul to follow her, "It's a dump. And it's not just a dump because you're a hopeless alcoholic, we'll talk about that later, but it's a dump because it is old, and it needs some love and care to return to it's former glory, to reach its potential, and it's not something we'll be able to do alone."

"What are you suggesting?"

"Well, we get some help. Maybe Denise, Achille and Raymond—"

"Not Raymond," Paul cut her off, "I still don't forgive him for shooting me."

"If I can forgive you, Paul, then you must forgive him too."

"Ok, fine, and Raymond."

"Good. And then we hire some Arabic boys from a town nearby. I've seen plenty drop into Denise's cafe, they're always looking for work. You work together with them, understand them, get to know them and most importantly, pay them what they deserve. And together we rebuild this villa, and we name it Vanessa, Villa Vanessa, in honour of your daughter and my girlfriend, and the beautiful thing is, it will be resurrected by the hand of the Arabs, the same people who you blame for taking her—"

"Will give her back to me," he finished her sentence. "It sounds a little cynical, don't you think?"

"Not at all, it sounds cynical to you because you've become cynical. That's the whole point in trying," she said, "to get you out of your rut."

"Yes, you're right. Ok then, when can we start?" he asked.

"Tomorrow?" Samia shrugged. "Before this whole dump collapses on our heads and kills us in our sleep."

"Great. And if we fail?" he looked at her.

"Then I return to Paris, and you never have to see me again."

<h1 style="text-align:center">16</h1>

Karim, Aziz and Fahad were brothers from the town of Cogolin, a popular village for migrants from the Arab world, in particular, Tunisia. Cogolin had once been a lively town, famous as the headquarters for the French liberation of Provence during the Second World War, but these days it was best described as tired, made up of working class families and far less glamorous than any of the neighbouring villages.

Karim, the eldest at nineteen, was an outgoing and easy-natured young man with a failed career as a footballer already under his belt. At just sixteen years old, his dream of playing for Olympique Marseille had looked all but set when he'd been drafted into their academy, but one unfortunate evening destroyed everything, when he'd gotten behind the wheel of his friend's car after a night of heavy drinking. Fortunately the crash hadn't killed anyone, but it had left him with his reputation destroyed and a broken leg that never quite healed right. Once out of hospital he was expelled from the academy and returned to Cogalin, where he spent his time floating between odd jobs with the hope of one day being a professional coach. Football was his life. His parents were deeply ashamed of his actions, but they'd forgiven him enough to allow him to return home.

Aziz, now eighteen and the most handsome of the three, was an aficionado of French hip-hop, and like his older brother he'd spend every minute he possibly could in Marseille. Only Aziz wasn't attending football games, but rather small hip-hop clubs, watching some of the best artists in the country make a name for themselves. He wrote songs furiously and had the dream of one day being on stage himself, although he never had the courage to show anyone his songs or perform in front of them. Unlike his brothers, Aziz felt more French than Tunisian, and while this upset his father it made his mother proud, for she too had found a friendlier life in France. Although he believed himself a socialist, Aziz hated hard work, and only took the job at Paul's villa because his brothers did and Paul promised to pay him well, better than any other white expat he'd met before, at least.

The third brother, Fahad, was the youngest at just fifteen years of age. Fahad identified strongly as being Tunisian, and refused to speak French when alone with his family. His dream was to save enough money in France and return to his homeland where he could start a family and work an honest job. He was staunchly Islamic, and he judged his two older brothers poorly for their hedonistic lifestyles, which he did not approve of. Still, he liked his brothers, and he was happy to take on the job with them, in order to put away a little bit more

money for that trip back across the Mediterranean towards home.

Raymond knew the boy's father well, for it was he
who'd been the head carpenter when Raymond had
had his home built some fifteen years earlier, and now
their father was thrilled to have his boys earn some decent money doing decent work.

Achille, a skilled tradesman who had once owned
the villa and allowed it to fall into disrepair, was forced
into his role as project manager by Denise. If he were to
refuse, she'd withhold sex for the entire summer. Achille
agreed to take it on without much deliberation.

One afternoon, in late May, they had a meeting at
Denise's cafe to discuss the plan, with Achille at the
head of the table and Paul and Raymond by his side.
Achille explained his plan in French, with Raymond
happy to sit quietly and drink, forever unwilling to
learn the language.

"Please, don't translate," he asked Samia, "the beauty of living in a country where you don't speak the language is not being able to understand the pointless shit
people say. It really is a blessing."

"But you won't understand the project," she objected.

"That's fine," he reassured her. "When we get down
there, you order me around all you like, I've always enjoyed being bossed around by beautiful women."

"Alright," Achille said, nervously glancing around
the table, "here is what I've decided. Paul, you will be
in charge of removing the old cement from the outside
of the villa and applying chalk where it once was. As
discussed this will allow the villa to breathe, and the
mould that is spreading inside will die off with time.

You'll be paired with Aziz, as he is the tallest of the brothers and there will be some hard to reach places."

Paul smiled at Aziz, who looked up from his phone for a moment and shook his head, before returning to a group chat with his friends.

"Denise, Raymond and Samia will work in the garden, repairing the fence and the path to the sea, while finishing off the work that has already started on the vines. When this has been finished, they will help Paul and Aziz paint the new chalk exterior."

Samia squeezed Denise's thigh under the table, she was excited to work outside with her in the late springtime air. Raymond, not understanding anything other than his name, smiled and took a swig of beer.

"Sounds like a plan," he said.

"Finally, I'll work with the other two brothers, Karim and Fahad, inside the villa," Achille continued. "We'll repair the walls and the damp in the ceiling. Then we'll patch up the floor in the kitchen and reapply all the shutters. If we work good hours and long hours," he went on, his nervousness having faded by now as he commanded his troops, "it should take no longer than three weeks. Any questions?"

"Yes," Karim said, raising his arm, "when will we get paid?"

"Paul will pay you at the end of each week," Samia answered, before Paul could open his mouth, "a hundred euros a day each for your trouble. If there's a delay on those payments, or if the amount is incorrect, come and see me and I'll make sure it's quickly fixed," she turned to Paul and smiled. "But I can't see that being a problem."

For the first few days of the restoration of the villa, Paul and Aziz worked on different sides of the house. The work was tiring and monotonous, chipping away at the old cement with a simple iron file under the glare of the unforgiving sun. All the men had opted to work with their shirts off, which didn't go unnoticed by Denise. Paul was lean and long, his torso still ripped with muscle, and of the three older men she found him the most pleasant to look at. Achille, meanwhile, by far the largest and hairiest of the lot, let his ample gut hang out over his faded blue jeans, while a steady stream of sweat flowed down his spine and settled in his backside. Raymond, his shoulders still strong and lean, had saggy pectoral muscles and a small gut that bounced when he laughed. He looked far younger than his seventy-eight years but still much older than Paul, who glistened in the sun, high up on his ladder as he chipped away at the house. As for the three brothers, well Denise chose not to look too closely, but they were all as she expected, lean and muscular and very beautiful. Samia, she noticed, looked most often towards Paul, and on many occasions Denise had caught her smiling at him.

Paul had tried to befriend Aziz, it was after all the purpose of the whole project, from Samia's perspective at least, but Aziz had little interest in befriending Paul. When Aziz arrived each morning, usually asleep in the back of Raymond's truck, he'd wake up and walk right past Paul and set up his ladder without saying a word. Once he was ready to work he'd put his headphones into his ears and leave them there until the day's shift was over. When Paul would try to start a conversation with him, Aziz would just grunt and put the music back on. Paul complained about this to Samia.

"He seems like a nice enough kid, and he's a good worker, but he isn't here to make friends."

"It's not about making friends Paul, surely Raymond is enough to turn you off having friends," she joked. "It's about respecting them."

"I do respect them," Paul said. "I'm trying to understand them, to understand what interests them, what gets them out of bed."

"I'll tell you what gets them out of bed—the latest football scores, the promise of a hundred euros they can spend on booze, a message from a lover they fell asleep texting. The chance to come here and steal glimpses of me, sweating in my singlet in the garden. The same things that get any teenage boy up. I'll tell you what doesn't get them up though—jihad."

"I have noticed Aziz keeps checking you out," Paul admitted.

"Jealous, are we?" she laughed.

"What would you say if I said I was?"

"I'd say you have the exact same taste as your daughter."

"Vanessa had very fine taste."

"Exactly," she teased.

Under Raymond's guidance, an excellent gardener with a photographic memory of his adventures through Africa, the garden began to come alive with palms and cactuses and brilliant flowering plants he'd bought at the market and had delivered by truck. Paul tried to give him money for the plants but he refused to accept it.

"As long as you let me do it my way, I'm happy to fork out the cash. Besides, if I can bring a little bit more of the jungle to France then I've done a good thing."

Inside the house, Achille directed the eldest and youngest brothers with expert guidance. The youngest, Fahad, even admitted to Achille one day that after the experience they were having, he wanted to become a builder himself. They were well ahead of schedule and were giving the interior a coat of paint while Paul and Aziz still applied the chalk layer to the exterior.

"Be careful," Paul said, his ladder alongside Aziz's, "the earth beneath is damp and the ladder might slip."

Aziz, his headphones in and his music blaring, didn't respond.

Meanwhile Denise, her joints aching from bending over in the garden, went inside the villa to see how Achille's work was progressing. She had noticed a fresh vitality in the normally disagreeable man, and it wasn't lost on her that it was inspired by the teenage boys he was teamed up with. If only he could be a father, she thought, he'd be a wonderful father. He'd teach his children to be strong like him, practical, hardworking. But alas, it could not be, and Denise accepted their fate and wished the renovation would go on for months rather than mere weeks, for Achille hadn't gambled once since the project had begun.

The smell off fresh tobacco wafted into the villa, as Raymond appeared behind Denise.

"So, what's going on in here then?" he asked, as he took his pipe out of his pocket and began packing it. "Bludging away in the cool while we burn alive in the blinding heat outside, I take it?"

Achille found Raymond to be arrogant and was glad they couldn't speak the same language, so he got Fahad's attention and asked asked him to follow him into the living room, where they were reinforcing the floorboards. But Karim, who imagined speaking English a necessary skill for a world-renowned football manager, took the opportunity to practice.

"Actually, Mr Raymond, I would prefer to be outside in the garden, where the smell from the paint is not so strong," he said. "In here it is hard to breathe."

"You're lying to me kid. You want to be out in the garden so you can stare at the girl. Don't worry, no one blames you for it."

Suddenly Denise elbowed Raymond in the ribs, causing his tobacco to spill from his palm.

"Back to work then, Raymond," she said.

"Oh, Denise, stop being so damn frigid. If he's not interested in Samia then there's a club in Saint-Tropez I can recommend him, needless to say you and the girl wouldn't be allowed in though," he laughed.

Denise shook her head and left the villa.

"Now," Raymond turned back to Karim, "want to know the story of this villa?"

The young man smiled and nodded.

"There was a murder suicide, two years ago. A couple of young lovers living off the grid. That nick on the wall behind you is where one of the bullets ricocheted. Not long after, Achille bought it cheap and then sold in on to Paul for peanuts. It was the worst decision Paul ever made, the place is cursed. Although, if he sells if after we fix it up he may make a nice profit."

Karim's smile faded, then he went to say something but as he did he heard a scream outside.

"Told ya," Raymond smiled.

17

While Denise and Raymond were inside the villa, speaking with Achille and Karim, Samia took the opportunity to take a break from the gardening and lay down to relax. As she made her way towards a shaded patch of grass, she turned to look at where Paul and Aziz were working, high up on their ladders, and was proud of Paul. Already, after just two weeks, the villa had been transformed and was glittering white in the afternoon sun. Next to the brilliant blue of the sea it looked like a sparkling stone in the pool of an enchanted fountain. Paul would be happy here, she thought, and so would she when she moved back in. As of yet there'd been no squabbles or petty arguments, and although Paul had complained that Aziz was insolent and guarded, she'd seen them engage in a few conversations over the past week and they seemed to be a little friendlier. If nothing else, at least Paul was trying.

As Samia sat in a nicely shaded spot with a view of the beach, she suddenly felt drawn to an area a few yards

away, hidden behind a small cleft of rocks and shrouded in weeds. She got to her feet and walked over and
noticed a small flowering plant, one she recognised although she wasn't sure why. It looked like an overgrown
succulent, with a swollen stem and prickly green leaves
which spiralled out from its wiry branches. There were
a half dozen flowers, pink and delicate, opening themselves towards the direction of the sun. It was a desert
rose, she realised, and all at once she felt a surge of emo-
tion swelling up in her chest.

Suddenly, a memory came back to her, she was with
Vanessa, on a trip they'd taken to Barcelona, just weeks
before she'd been killed.

"Follow me," Vanessa had said, "I want to show you
something."

Vanessa led Samia though the alleys of the gothic
quarter and out towards Las Ramblas. The previous
evening the girls had gotten so drunk together that
they'd snuck into a charming, old apartment building
and made their way up to its rooftop terrace. On the
rooftop there was a mattress left out to dry and some
sheets on the clothesline. Vanessa flipped the mattress
to the floor and laid the sheets out over it. Then she undressed and invited Samia to join her. She did. After
some time they'd made too much noise in their feverish lovemaking and someone below began shouting at
them, then they dressed as quickly as possible and ran
out of the building laughing like mad people. They continued drinking long into the night, until just before the
sun rose, and now as they walked through the gothic
quarter Samia's hangover felt paralysing.

"This better be good," she said, "all I want to do is sleep."

"Stop whinging, it's just over here and then we'll return to the hotel," Vanessa responded, leading Samia by her hand.

Las Ramblas was packed full of people on a vibrant Sunday afternoon. The girls kept walking until Vanessa found the store she was looking for, it was a florist.

"This is the plant I want to buy you," she said, picking one up from a small table. "It's called a desert rose, see?" she said, pointing to its tag. "The name makes me think of you, you're my rose from the desert in Algeria," she smiled.

"And you're my rose from the desert in Australia," Samia laughed.

They kissed.

Vanessa had bought the plant for Samia, and Samia had looked after it until the attack had taken her lover away. It wasn't long after until the plant had died too.

Samia knelt next to the plant in the garden. She reached out and softly touched a petal, hoping that maybe Vanessa had sent her there. That's stupid, Samia thought to herself, of course she hadn't, but at the same time she desperately hoped that she had. "Hi Ness," she said, as a sad smile crossed her face. She could feel tears begin to sting her eyes when suddenly she heard a scream behind her. She recognised the voice as Paul's, and her moment vanished as quickly as it had appeared.

Samia ran over to where Paul was laying on the ground, grunting in the mud. His limbs awkwardly twisted around him.

"What happened?" Samia asked, kneeling down beside him.

"Nothing," Paul groaned through clenched teeth, "I

slipped, that's all."

"He tried to push me," Aziz shouted from above, still high on his ladder. "He tried to fuck with me!"

"What?" Samia turned back to Paul. "Is this true?" she asked, as Denise and Raymond gathered around them.

"Of course it isn't true," Paul muttered, "I was trying to warn him that his ladder wasn't steady but of course he wasn't listening. He never listens. Then he began to slip and I reached to grab him and I'm the bloody one who fell," he groaned.

"Why should I listen to you?" Aziz shouted down. "You're not even the boss."

"I'm the one who's bloody paying you," Paul muttered, as Raymond helped Paul up so he was sitting.

"Let me get some wine," Denise said, as she rushed inside, "wine is the only cure after a fall."

"Paul, are you ok?" Samia asked, ignoring Aziz as he argued with Achille.

Paul moved his legs back and forth, lifted his arms over his head and turned his neck. "I think I'm fine," he said at last, "better than I was when Raymond shot me, at least."

"Hmm," Raymond grunted, "I thought all that was behind us."

"It won't be behind us until I get to shoot you back," Paul said.

"All's fair in love and war," Raymond agreed.

As Denise returned from the house with a bottle of wine, which she insisted Paul drink despite his own objections, Aziz climbed down the ladder and stormed away from the group and headed towards the beach.

Samia chased after him.

"Aziz," she shouted, "wait for me."

Aziz stopped short of the sand and sat on the rocks. The sky became overcast as she knelt down beside him, both of their gazes fixed to the sea.

"Why are you so angry?" she asked him, studying his face. She still thought him good looking despite his rage.

"Why not, I'm sick of his bullshit, and then he falls and blames me."

"But he didn't blame you, Aziz, he said he slipped."

"It was the way he said it."

"Well, was it your fault?"

"What if it was? He is always bossing me around, looking at me like I am less than him. Just because he has the money it doesn't mean he owns me, I know he thinks like this. Like all white men."

"It is complicated, Aziz, he is trying his best to understand you, but you listen to music all day and ignore him. Then he becomes frustrated."

"So what if I want to listen to music, I never wanted this dumbass job, my father forced me into it."

"Just think of the money."

"Money is for motherfuckers. I'm an artist, money doesn't mean shit to me," he snapped.

"Paul is an artist too, he was very famous once," she told him.

"That man doesn't know a thing about art. To make art you have to suffer, when has a rich bastard like him ever suffered?"

Samia stood up and turned away from Aziz, she found him too stubborn and immature to deal with, like all the men she met his age. Everything he was saying was nonsense, and she felt that maybe her plan hadn't been a great idea after all. She went to walk away but decided she had to say one more thing.

"Aziz," she said, stealing his attention from the sea, "Paul's wife died when she was still young, and then his daughter was killed in the terrorist attacks in Paris last year. That man *has* suffered."

She walked away and left Aziz alone, the both of them fuming.

18

When Achille hammered the final nail into the last loose floorboard in the kitchen, it had been three full weeks since the renovation had begun. All that was left to do was a second coat of paint in the living room and the villa would be complete. Karim and Fahad, as enthusiastic about the project as ever, assured Achille they'd get it done before sunset as they were both eager to join the party planned for that evening, Karim secretly hoping to steal a few drinks. It was a party to celebrate the rebirth of the villa, Villa Vanessa.

Raymond and Samia were applying the finishing touches to the chalk exterior as Paul, his back too stiff to work any longer, got a guided tour through the garden with a very proud Denise. The place looked beautiful, a private paradise by the sea, the kind of place he would be able to sit peacefully and think. The kind of place where he could design a new life for himself, a new perspective, a new future. A future away from the pain and agony of his past life, his past life which had defined him, but would define him no more. Perhaps a home for Samia too, where she could be free of the agony that had crippled her in Paris. A Paris she thought she loved, but was realising quickly, no longer existed in the way it once had. He thanked Denise for her hard work and promised to pay her back someday.

"Don't thank me," she said, "thank my chef, Pierre. Had he not helped out these last two weeks there's no chance I could have been away from the cafe so long. To be honest, I've enjoyed the break."

Paul smiled, and looked back towards the house. He saw the two ladders lined up beside one another on the grassy slope and he thought of Aziz, he wondered how he must be feeling. After Paul had fallen off the ladder, Aziz had chosen not to return to work on the villa. Paul thought it was because the boy must have hated him, but in actuality, Aziz was ashamed of the way he'd behaved, especially after what Samia had told him. Still, Paul sent home with his brothers the full three weeks pay he'd promised him at the beginning, despite him having quit early and deserving only two-thirds.

When Denise and Paul returned to the villa they found Samia sitting with Raymond and Achille in the gentle gaze of the sun. The three of them looked exhausted, but at ease.

"We're done," Samia beamed, unable to stop smiling. "Welcome to your new home, old man," she laughed, her eyes fixed to his.

"It's your home too, Samia, if you want to return."

"I'll think about it, although I've discovered the advantages of living above a bar are numerous and hard to resist."

"And I'm not ready to give her up just yet," Denise chimed in. "I've gotten used to sleeping-in every morning."

Paul smiled, and thought he felt real happiness for the first time in months. "I can't thank you all enough..." he started, before Raymond cut him off.

"Paul, shut up would you. I'm an old man, as are you and Achille too, and old men have no time for sentimentality. The afternoon is short and the bottles are still full, so let the women be sentimental and let the men drink," he declared as he raised his glass. "To the death of sentimentality," he toasted.

"And to the birth of Villa Vanessa," Samia joined in.

"I think you two are toasting opposite things," Paul observed.

"Just be quiet and drink," Raymond demanded, as Denise handed Paul a glass of wine.

Later that afternoon, once the two remaining brothers had finished applying a fresh coat of white paint to the living room, Denise set up a table in the garden near the cliff face and the poplar tree. Not long after, Achille returned from a trip into town, where he'd collected some food from the cafe that Pierre had prepared for them. He spread out across the table a feast of fresh bread, local cheese, sardines, anchovies, olives and fresh fruit. As they sat down to eat they all took turns complimenting the villa, and all were optimistic about their futures. Especially Paul. Everything was perfect, apart from the ominous clouds now gathering on the horizon, threatening to spoil the party with a mighty storm.

Being near the cliff face, Paul couldn't help but remember his madness a couple of short weeks ago, right where they were now sitting down to eat. He was disturbed to recall how close he'd come to actually doing it, to actually jumping. He looked at Raymond, sitting opposite him now, and recalled an evening they'd spent together many years earlier in the Congo, when Raymond, drunk on the misfortune of a lover's sigh gone wrong, had threatened to do the same off the edge of the Inga Falls. It must happen to everyone, Paul thought, everyone must have their moment on the edge, but only some choose to jump, while some choose to die slowly. Paul knew now he'd be one to die slowly, but what of the others? The early evening sun, still present despite the clouds, was invigorating and Paul was glad to have made the decision he did. He looked at Samia, sipping on a glass of white wine, and she made him realise that life had some potential yet, and perhaps Paul Greene wasn't quite as forsaken as he'd feared.

"Samia, would you come for a walk?" he asked her, trying to be as inconspicuous as possible.

"Where to?" she asked.

"The top of the hill, I want to show you how to take a photo as the sun sets, how to capture the light just perfectly."

"Oh dear," she said as she slowly got up from her chair, "I wasn't aware photography 101 was this afternoon, had I known I might not have drunk so much."

"You'll be fine," Raymond reassured her, "you could spend a lifetime going through Paul's portfolio and you wouldn't find a single decent picture taken sober."

As Samia and Paul walked away from the table, Raymond, who was now surrounded by people who barely spoke English, tipped his hat down over his eyes and tried to get some sleep. He'd been feeling unwell since the renovation began, and he already felt the evening slipping away from him as the dreaded drowsiness set in. Paul and Samia had been acting mysteriously, he'd noticed, something between them had changed and he couldn't help but feel a little jealous. Oh well, he thought, Paul's bound to screw it up somehow. What a couple of old fools they'd become, he laughed to himself. What a couple of miserable old fools.

At the top of the hill, which looked over the villa and the sea, Paul and Samia stopped as Paul took out his camera.

"First," he said, "let me adjust the settings."

"Ok," she replied, as she watched on, the strap blowing in the cool breeze.

"There's no perfect way to shoot a sunset," he told her, as he put the viewfinder up to his eye, "but it's fun to experiment with the exposure and the focal length. The rule of thirds is especially important," he went on, "when photographing the sea and the sky together."

"Paul," Samia said, as he played around with the Leica.

"Yes?" he asked.

"That's not why you brought me here, anyone can point a lens at that view, at this time of day, and take a beautiful picture. I'm not an idiot," she said, her eyes burning into his.

"I know you're not," he conceded as he lowered the camera. She looked radiant in the orange glow, her mouth fixed in a coy smile and her eyelashes dancing on the breeze. "I suppose I wanted to thank you," he said, "away from all the others."

"For what?" she asked.

"For being so patient with me, for reaching out in the first place. For taking care of Vanessa and loving her when she was so far from me."

"That's it? You wanted to thank me?"

"Yes, I mean, no. Well, actually I don't know. Thank you for introducing me to the boys, they can be little shits, especially Aziz, but I can see now they are the same as any other boy their age. They're not all maniacs like I imagined them to be, lost, maybe, but extreme—no, of course not. I was a fool to ever think like that."

"So you don't think we're all terrorists, then?" she laughed.

"No, absolutely not. I mean I never did, except for maybe a moment or two, when everything went dark. I mean it's hard, isn't it?"

"It is hard," she agreed, "and hate is easy."

"Hate is very easy," Paul nodded. "Hate is like getting drunk on cheap wine, it tastes good, and the more you have the easier it is to drink. And it costs you next to nothing. But you wake up in the morning feeling like hell. If you wake up at all, that is."

He stared into her eyes and she stared back, neither of them able nor wanting to break away. She looked as beautiful as he'd ever seen her, as beautiful as he'd ever seen any woman. Her lips trembled a little as her breath grew short and Paul noticed for the first time translucent flecks of green in her deep brown eyes. He edged closer to her, and she to him, and he felt like touching her as she tilted her face towards his. Her precious face, which his daughter had once loved, so close to him now, her lips so close to his lips. So close to Vanessa. Vanessa's lips. Then something changed, something didn't feel right, and he pulled away.

"Shall we go back down, then?" he mumbled, as he forced his eyes away from hers. She looked at him, confused, why had he broken the moment? Why had he ruined something so perfect? "I'll go join the others, and I'll see you when you're ready," he said, as he started walking back down the hill towards the villa. Samia remained behind, not understanding what had just happened, while Paul cursed himself with every step that took him further from her.

"Remember to adjust the exposure," he called out to her behind him. She remained still, dejected. Then he turned back to himself and muttered, "You fool, Paul."

19

When Aziz had informed his father he wouldn't be returning with his brothers to complete the work on the villa, his father, Mohamed, was furious.

"How can you give up on your duties so easily?" he shouted at his son in Arabic.

"Because it's all bullshit, father," his son replied, deflecting the blame from himself.

"And now you swear at me. What in Allah's name have I done to deserve this?" he cried.

"If you listen to me you'll understand," his son pleaded. "Just listen for once."

"Fine, go on then," Mohamed instructed.

Aziz told his father how Paul had seemed strange at first, distant towards him, disinterested even. This suited Aziz just fine, as he took the job to make money, not to make friends. However, he noticed that Paul only made an effort to talk to him when Samia, the beautiful Algerian, was watching.

"He's in love with this girl, father, it is no good, the

girl is far too young for him!"

He told his father about the incident on the ladder, when Paul had pushed him and so he pushed back, and about the conversation he had with Samia on the rocks.

"The whole thing was a ploy, an act, orchestrated by her. You see his daughter was killed in Paris, and now he is a racist, and this makes the Algerian girl angry. They used us, father."

Mohamed dismissed his son and sat down to think about what he'd told him. While it seemed almost certain that his sons had been used for a purpose, was it not for a good purpose? Was it not better that this man, ignorant before, had now become enlightened? Allah was, if nothing else, all-forgiving. Mohamed decided he'd have to speak to the man himself, and the Algerian girl too, but he'd wait until the boys had finished their work. It was, after all, good work, and they had paid his sons handsomely. Although Aziz would have to return all of the money he hadn't earned.

As Paul returned from the conversation with Samia on the hill, which had left him more confused than he'd been in years, he was surprised to see that Aziz had joined the group, as well as an older man Paul took to be the boy's father.

"Paul," Raymond called over his shoulder, his face partially protected from the sun by his hat, "there's someone you ought to meet."

Mohamed, a gentle, older man with a dark grey moustache and a balding head, was excited to meet Paul, the man who'd given his sons the opportunity to understand the merits of hard work. He extended his hand to greet him and they shook enthusiastically.

"You have been very kind to all three of my boys," Mohamed said in English, his accent sounded almost musical to Paul.

"No, not at all," Paul responded vacantly, his thoughts still lost with Samia on the hill. "Your boys are wonderful men, excellent workers too, it would have been impossible to do any of this without them," he complimented Mohamed.

Aziz, who had remained quiet until now, stepped forward to say something but just as quickly his father motioned for him to remain silent.

"That is not all true, Mr. Greene, as I understand Aziz here was not of much use."

"Actually," Paul responded, "Aziz was very useful, he chipped off half the cement from the villa himself, I wouldn't have been able to complete it alone. It's not easy work, especially with the sun we've been having. After forty-five minutes on that ladder one's head begins to spin, let alone six hours."

The sun had been brilliant those last two weeks, hot and high like the suns of summer, only it was still spring. In fact the entire springtime had been hot and dry, and the drought was causing major concerns for everyone from the farmers to the winemakers. "The whole region," Raymond had observed weeks earlier, "is a tinderbox waiting to explode."

"Can I say something, father?" Aziz asked, his eyes downcast and his hands deep in his pockets, fingering loose coins.

"Please, speak," his father commanded.

"Well," Aziz said as he looked up and noticed Samia,

the beautiful Algerian girl who kept him awake at night, approaching the party.

"Well?" his father prompted him.

"Well," he continued, "I just wanted to say thank you, Mr. Greene, you were very kind to us. And I'm sorry about your daughter, but it wasn't our fault."

"I'm sorry?" Paul said.

"Your daughter," Aziz went on, "the one who'd got blown up, excuse me, killed, I'm sorry that happened."

"How do you know about my daughter?" Paul asked, as Raymond and Denise sat up to listen more closely. Paul glanced at Samia, who was by his side now. She went to say something but hesitated. "Did you tell them?" he asked her, his eyes looked frightening, she thought.

"Just Aziz, not the others," she stammered.

"You didn't think that maybe it was my business to share that?" he snapped.

"Let it go, Paul," Raymond butted in, "the cat's out of the bag, no use hiding from it."

"Hiding from it?" Paul repeated his friend. "How do you know what I'm hiding from Raymond? You, who's been hiding from the world for the last thirty years is now dishing out accusations?"

Raymond made a dismissive gesture with his hand and turned away, wishing they'd go back to speaking in French so he could sit in peace.

"I'm sorry, Mr. Greene," Mohamed interrupted, "my son should not have spoken of things he does not yet understand."

"No, it's fine, your son can speak all he likes, in fact

I'm surprised to find he has a voice, I did after all waste two weeks trying to talk to him. It's Samia though, who has a problem saying things she shouldn't. And Raymond too, of course, who's never known how to keep his mouth shut for more than a minute."

"Paul," Samia pleaded, "I'm sorry, I didn't know it was a secret, don't forget she belonged to me too."

"At least someone talks about her, Paul," Raymond added, his back still turned to them, "you mentioned her once and never again. People die a second time when they're no longer remembered."

Paul turned and glared at his old friend, and he felt as if he were under interrogation for the crime of not having loved his daughter enough.

"Have any of you lost a child before?" Paul asked the group. Raymond remained still as Denise shook her head. Achille stood up and collected some plates, he walked back towards the villa, finding the mood too tense and the English impossible to understand.

"It doesn't make for light conversation," Paul continued, "believe it or not. It's not the first thing you tell someone when you're introduced to them. But Raymond's right, he always is—the cat's out of the bag so let me tell you what happened. After the explosion, after she was blown up as Aziz so eloquently put it, and once the heat had died down, they were unable to find Vanessa's body, just parts of it. Parts of her amongst the parts of countless other people, and a badly burnt passport in the back pocket of a piece of thigh. That's how we were sure she'd died, that single piece of thigh. It took them so long to get down into those tunnels after the explosions that rats had already began to feast on what remained. It was an unidentifiable mess of human blood and shit. The police didn't tell me any of this, of course not, they don't tell you anything, they apologise and post the passport back to you once they're done photographing it for evidence. Instead I read about it online, I read about a lot of things online, you become addicted to the things you read, the things you're told. It's like hip hop for you, Aziz, or Africa for Raymond, or gambling for Achille, it becomes all you have. It becomes an obsession. You see, the people who talk to you online have also lost their children, or their wives or husbands, unlike all of you. And they understand, Samia, that one doesn't simply own the dead, no one owns the dead, except maybe the rats who ingest them, maybe they own them, but no one else. As you stay online you dig deeper, and you understand things that you weren't supposed to. You learn about ISIS, you learn about the Middle East, you learn about the Quran. You begin to learn, Mohamed, how otherwise decent boys like your own become radicalised, become dangerous. How they fill themselves with enough hate to murder sweet and innocent young women like Vanessa, Samia's Vanessa, how they sacrifice girls like her to the rats. I'm sorry I used you Aziz, and your brothers, but it served a purpose. I can see now that what I read was bullshit, all of it, but when you can't talk about something you learn to listen, and you listen to the voices which are the loudest. I wanted to keep Vanessa's murder a secret, but I suppose now you know."

Paul's speech drifted off as the group remained silent,

he reached for his wine and began to move away from them. "It doesn't matter, none of it matters," he said, with a wave of his hand. "If anyone needs me I'll be at the beach. But please don't need me, just leave me be."

"Mr. Greene," Mohamed spoke up before Paul had left, "I am moved by your speech, but if you'll allow me, I'd like to add something."

"Go ahead," Paul said, his back still turned to the group.

"While it's true, I haven't lost a child, I am not without my own pain. My brother, also named Aziz, was killed by an American drone in Syria, volunteering to help those desperate people who are like brothers and sisters to us. And my niece, also a great beauty like your daughter and Samia, drowned crossing the Mediterranean two years ago. She could have been saved, but the captain of the ship that passed them wouldn't waste the petrol needed to turn back. It would be easy for me to hate the west, to hate the French, the Americans, the Russians, to hate the world. But it serves no good, for not all men are alike. Those young men, who took your daughter, did not do so in the name of Allah, but in contempt of him."

Mohamed walked over to Paul and put his hand on his shoulder.

"Whatever thoughts you may have had, Allah forgives you," he said.

Paul rubbed Mohamed's hand, and then turned and hugged him. He looked to where Samia stood, beside Raymond, and noticed tears in her eyes. He'd never seen actual tears in her eyes before.

"Please, continue your party, I just need a moment

alone," he said, pulling back from Mohamed. He took
a full bottle of wine from the table and made his way to
the beach. Samia looked at Raymond, who shook his
head, and then she followed after Paul.

20

As Samia approached the beach, a gentle rain blew across the breeze and dampened her brow. She raised a hand to her forehead and shielded her eyes from the tiny droplets as she paused for a moment to marvel at the view. The storm was now gathering pace on the horizon, it had been brewing all day, as fiery shrieks of lightening waged war against the tumultuous sea. It appeared to be moving towards her, albeit slowly and waywardly, and so she didn't feel the need to panic. Not yet, at least. The air was hot and fragrant, and she enjoyed the taste of the salt that floated upon it. It made her think of Vanessa, who was enamoured by the sea, so much so that Samia always imagined she could taste it on her skin.

Evening was approaching fast and the mood was ominous. The water, in sync with its surroundings, grew restless and cruel as it so often did on the peninsula. The cape, shrouded in mist, vanished from view like a phantom ship. Samia spied Paul, just, as he sat alone on the railing of the ruined cottage, his feet dug into the sand

and his arms wrapped tightly around himself. She approached him purposefully but slowly. She could sense he was still mad at her.

"The boy is in love with you," Paul said as she reached him and settled down beside him. "I could see it in his eyes. No wonder he hated me so much."

Samia smiled. "Can you blame him?" she teased.

Paul shifted around and faced her, she seemed to him so fragile in the elements. The wind flung her hair across her face and caused her eyes to squint so tightly her lashes met. He reached over and removed a strand of her hair that was caught in her lips. He wanted to stay angry, but seeing her so delicate he couldn't help but love her. She smiled as his hand brushed against her cheek. He was gentle, and she was glad.

"Of course not," he said, turning back to face the beach, "I'd worry about anyone who wasn't in love with you. I'd have their pulse checked, their brain examined."

Samia laughed. "Do you find me beautiful, Paul?" she asked, trying not to sound too brash.

"You know I do."

"That's all, though, isn't it?"

"No," he shook his head, "of course not. There's plenty more to you."

"Like what?"

"Well, you're intelligent, to start with. You have empathy, I mean you must since you're a nurse. You also have a depth I find refreshing."

"A depth?"

"Yes. I notice it because I have none myself. If I am a puddle then you are an ocean."

She laughed again.

"What?" he protested.

"I'm sorry Paul, that just sounds so sentimental. You are never sentimental."

"Everyone gets sentimental when it storms," he observed.

"There you go again," she laughed. "No, Paul, sentimental men don't behave like you. Besides, you must have depth, you are an artist, after all."

"My photos were never art, they were documents, a record. Nothing more."

She sat silent for a moment and thought about what he'd said. She didn't agree, Vanessa had shown her his photos many times, photos of models and animals and landscapes, all of them unusual. They were beautiful, she thought. Intelligent too. Paul was definitely an artist.

"If you could record this moment," she asked as she shifted closer to him, her arm now pressed against his, "how would you do it?"

"What do you mean?"

"Well, if you could record this moment, right now, you and I watching the storm gather pace. Would you do it with a song, a photograph, a poem?"

Paul thought for a moment, how would he record it? The scenery was spectacular, so it would have to be visual, but the elements were electric, so it would need to be heard. A film, perhaps? Forget it, he thought, what a stupid question. Moments like this can't be recorded, they can only be lived, and then relived in the mind's eye. Again and again and again—until death.

And so he kissed her.

Samia liked being kissed, probably more than anything else in the world, and Paul, she was pleased to discover, was a good kisser. Just like Vanessa had been.

Paul pulled at her hips and swung her around until she was in front of him, her lips were locked to his and her arms gripped tightly around his neck. He reached around and felt her body, her thighs, the small of her back. In return she felt him, his shoulders, his biceps, the nape of his neck. Paul was strong, she realised, she felt it as he tugged at her. She'd thought wrongly because of his age that he'd be weak. It was a pleasant surprise. He lifted her top over her head and whispered as he chewed at her ear.

"Meet me in the sea."

And she did. They swam together as the sea attempted to swallow them whole. It was a moonless night but the lighthouse was alive. On each rotation it kept them warm and safe, safe in each others arms. After unknown hours she followed him back to the villa, and neither of them were surprised to discover that everyone else had packed up and left. She joined him in the shower where they warmed each other up, their hands lathering and massaging and pushing the other against the glass. Then, as she joined him in the bed, the sky went black while the incessant thunder, like the toll of a bell, drowned out her moans.

Later, much later, in the stillness which followed, they were both surprised to discover tears in their eyes. Were they tears for Vanessa? For the dead lover and the dead daughter? Were they tears of happiness or guilt or confusion? Neither of them knew. Neither of them had the courage to ask. Then, as they laid there, lost in their thoughts, a bolt of lightening cracked right above the villa and lit up the room with a brilliant white light. For a moment she could see him and was reminded of his sadness, and he of her beauty, and they pulled the other closer in an act of desperation. They remained like that, perfectly still, uncertain and scared of the storm which now hounded them like wolves.

"Paul," Samia whispered, her head nestled into his chest, "I don't feel well."

"I can get you some water," he said.

"No, I mean, I feel fine, I just feel bad."

"Because of what happened?"

"I guess so. I don't know. How do you feel?"

"I don't know."

"We shouldn't have done it."

"What's done is done. It's what happens next that matters."

"We never talk about her. Why do we never talk about her?"

"Because what can we say, that we miss her? That we wish she hadn't died? That we want her back? Her dying delivered you to me and me to you and that's about the only solace we'll ever get from the whole damn mess. Let's be glad for that, even if it is just tonight."

"Ok," she said, as she tried again to sleep. After a few minutes of silence she asked him if the storm would pass.

"Unlikely, we're stuck in the middle of it now, that's why it's so quiet."

"But it's not even raining," she observed as she braved a look out the window. She was saddened to see the garden getting torn apart in the wind. She'd worked so hard in that garden so Paul could find some peace. Paul would never know peace, would he? And what of the desert rose? Had that been destroyed too?

"What if something happens?" she wondered aloud. "What if it gets worse?"

"Then I'll look after you as best I can, and you'll have to look after me. I am an old man, don't forget."

"How could I forget," she smiled, as she reclined back into his arms. "Although you don't seem old, not tonight, at least."

Paul looked into her eyes, barely visible in the dark, as she looked into his. "The damage is done, isn't it?" he asked.

"It is, very much so."

"But the night isn't, is it?"

"Not at all," she agreed.

"Then let's spend it as if it were our last on earth, which it very may well be if things outside don't settle down," he proposed, as a shutter bashed against the bedroom window, before being torn away and flying off towards the hill.

"Let's," she agreed, as she kicked her legs out from under the covers and mounted him.

While the lovers, old and young, were locked in their embrace, Raymond, back at his own house, locked his balcony doors and pulled down the blinds. He'd seen storms like this before and they never ended well. The mix of drought ravaged land and dry lightening was a recipe for carnage, and he wondered if he should drive down to the cape and warn the couple.

To hell with them, he thought, it's not like they're driving out here to check on me, is it? Nothing wrong with a little adventure.

And so, feeling confident his own house was secure enough to survive the night, Raymond laid down to sleep. But he didn't sleep, as an uneasy feeling in his stomach ate away at him, an uneasy feeling which told him his friends weren't safe out on that peninsula, so close to the sea, not safe at all. If the storm got any worse he'd have to climb in his truck and rescue them.

"Alright then," he mumbled, as he swung his legs off the bed and planted his feet in his slippers. He looked at the clock, it was four in the morning. His back ached worse than it ever had before, and in the dark he fumbled around for a walking cane before getting to his feet. He left his bedroom and walked over to the balcony doors and raised the blind.

Raymond pressed his hands to the glass, as the howling winds screamed like wounded harpies, and he thought he could see a glimmer of light coming from the direction of the cape. He went back to his bedroom and put on his reading glasses, then he returned to the balcony to see more clearly.

"Shit," he muttered under his breath, his raspy voice matching the timbre of the thunder, "the whole goddamn peninsula's on fire."

21

Raymond flew his truck around the bends with reckless abandon and impressive skill. The canopy of oaks above him swirled with fury while behind him, in his rearview mirror, he could just make out a tree collapsing across the street. A brilliant jolt of lightning lit up the road as debris flung in front of him in every possible direction.

"Goddamnit," he shouted as he tried to control his vehicle against the thrust of the wind. If only it were raining, he thought, then the storm wouldn't be such an issue, a few trees would fall and a house here and there might lose a roof, but at least the headland wouldn't burn.

In the dark he sped through the village and down the slopes toward the sea. As he approached the peninsula he could see the billowing smoke rise higher and engulf the sky. The moon, barely visible, was a harrowing red. He'd been saying for months now that a storm like this would spell catastrophe, but no one listened, no one ever did. He should have warned Paul at least, he thought, his friend had no idea of the perils of living so close to that damn forest.

As he approached the villa the smoke grew so thick it was almost hidden out of view. The driveway, flanked either side by bush, was inaccessible as the wind thrust torrents of flames back and forth across it. He did a hook turn to the right, where the flames hadn't yet reached, and catapulted the truck over a ditch and down a ravine towards the house. Had he been paying closer attention he might have heard the fuel containers rattling around in the back of his flat-bed, but he hadn't. For a moment he almost lost control as he tilted the truck onto the two right wheels, before he righted it again and pulled up just outside the villa. All around him flames swirled, but he was relieved to see the villa hadn't yet been consumed. There was hope for them yet. He climbed out of his vehicle and bashed at the door before trying the handle and letting himself in.

"Paul!" he shouted as he entered the kitchen, "Samia!"

He charged through the house towards the bedroom and flung open the door, the covers were strewn on the floor and the bed was empty. He went into the living room and was alarmed to find it empty too.

"Where the bloody hell are you?" he muttered through clenched teeth.

As Raymond exited the villa he was disturbed to find the flames were approaching his truck. It was now that he remembered the petrol tanks, and so he ran over and jumped in the front seat, desperate to get it out of harms way before it caught fire and exploded. He was too late, the flames had already caught up to it. In a last, demented effort he directed the truck towards the cliffs and released the handbrake, then he leapt out of the rolling vehicle and bolted.

Raymond Bishop, seventy eight years old with a broken body and ruined legs, wearing nothing but a night gown and flimsy cotton slippers, ran as fast as he had ever run in his life. He charged away from the villa, away from the burning truck, along the only route that wasn't yet blocked by fire, the route to the beach.

Paul and Samia, having taken shelter just minutes earlier in the old shack by the sea, were both bowled over by the blast. The truck and its two spare containers of fuel sent a fireball twenty feet wide and thirty feet high into the air.

"The villa," Paul cried as he climbed to his feet. "You must be joking?"

"Paul, no," Samia shouted as he began to run along the sand towards it, "please Paul, stay with me."

Paul couldn't hear her pleas, he couldn't hear anything with the blast of the truck still rattling in his ears. He charged along the sand and up the rocks until the flames blocked his way with a wall of impossibly intense heat.

Suddenly an arm pulled at him and he shrugged it off.

"Paul, let's go," Samia pleaded, her voice becoming desperate.

Paul remained dejected, he remained still. He didn't move, he didn't turn to look at her, instead he just stood there, mute and paralysed, as he watched his home burn.

"Paul!" Samia cried, still tugging at him. "Please let's go!"

Around them clouds of embers spun in vicious little

spirals and landed in their hair. Samia shrieked in pain as she batted them away but Paul didn't react. She tried to pull at him again but this time he swung his arm out, unwittingly striking her across the face. She collapsed behind him on the rocks and began sobbing. Then, out of nowhere, a figure approached Paul and struck him across the jaw with a mighty right hook. Paul stumbled back and collapsed onto his rear, his eyes still fixed on the flames.

"Samia," Raymond shouted over the roaring fire, "you take his arms and I'll get his legs. He's in shock and we need to get him out of harms way before the flames eat him alive."

Samia and Raymond lugged Paul across the sand and away from danger, away from the ruined villa and towards the cabin just back from the sand. The cabin was far enough away from the fire to remain safe for the night, and when they reached it Samia kicked open the door and they sprawled Paul out on the dusty floor. There was an empty bucket in the corner and Samia grabbed it and rushed to the sea, she filled it with water and hurried back to the two men.

"Here," she said as she passed the water to Raymond, "he has some burns from the embers, we need to cool them."

Raymond looked at the girl, who was shaking with fright. "You also have burns," he noticed, "come here, we'll look after you first."

Samia knelt in front of Raymond as he dampened a cloth and wiped down her neck and shoulders. The salt in the water stung her, but she remained perfectly still.

"Why are you here?" she asked. "Why aren't you at

home?"

"I woke up and saw the flames coming along the coast. I got here as quick as I could but it was too late."

"What was the explosion?" she asked.

"It was my truck, I blew up the villa," he admitted, his eyes downcast. "I feel lousy as hell." He noticed her shaking, and became worried. "What's wrong?" he asked.

"It was Vanessa," she whispered, her eyes welling up.

"What?"

"The villa. We named it after Vanessa, and now it's gone. It's as if she's died a second time," she said, as she stroked Paul's forehead with wet fingers.

"Don't think of it like that," Raymond tried to calm her, "think of it as a rebirth. You know the story of the phoenix? Rising out of the flames? Think of it like that."

Outside the window Samia could hear the howling fury of the fire as it grew higher and higher and inched closer to them.

"It's a pretty horrible rebirth," she said, before she laid down beside Paul and tried her best to rest.

A few hours later Raymond woke the two of them, and was glad to find Paul responsive again.

"There's people coming down the ridge," Raymond observed, "they look like emergency crews, time to get up and get the hell out of here."

A team of three firefighters had braved the flames to search the beach for survivors. When they reached the cabin they applied first aid to the three wounded friends, before guiding them up a back route which avoided the lingering flames, which by now had mostly been extinguished.

Back in town Raymond gave a statement to the police, explaining his rescue effort and consequent explosion, and then he went to join Paul and Samia, now officially homeless, who had checked into rooms above Denise's cafe. Samia was upstairs asleep, while Paul sat alone at the bar with a coffee. Raymond, having been home and back to change out of his night robe, approached Paul slowly.

"I don't feel too great," he said as he sat down.

"Don't worry about it," Paul replied. "You were only trying to help."

"I was, and the villa probably would have burnt away anyhow, those flames were damn close."

"Yes, I remember," Paul said, "when the two of us decided to run they were just meters away. It all happened so quickly."

"All that matters is the two of you are safe."

Paul took a sip of his coffee and stared at his reflection in the mirrored glass behind the bar. He saw a broken man. A man as broken as any man he'd ever seen before.

"What's your next move then?" Raymond asked, sensing something had changed in his friend.

"Get the hell out of here, I suppose. Maybe I can sell off the land but it might be smart to wait until it's stopped burning. Then I'll catch a train to Italy or Spain and do my best to forget about it. Forget the girl, forget you, forget everything."

"I have no qualms about you forgetting me Paul, but don't talk about the girl like that. It'll break her heart."

"She needs her heart broken."

"What do you mean by that?"

"What I mean is I'm in love with her Raymond, and if I stick around then she may end up falling in love with me too. What good will that do? In ten years I'll be al-most seventy and she'll only be thirty-five. Five years later she'll be wiping my ass because I can't do it myself. What's the point in putting her through any of that?"

"You know, Paul, I am seventy nine this year, and I think you'll be interested to know I still wipe my own ass just fine."

"I don't doubt it, Raymond," Paul said as he turned and faced his friend, "but we're different, you and I. You keep on going because you don't know what else to do, but I'm slowing down as I can't see the point of any of it anymore. The girl needs to forget about me and the sooner I let that happen the easier it'll be for everyone."

"You're talking through your ass Paul, sleep on it a few days would you?"

The two of them went quiet for a few minutes, unsure of what conversation the moment demanded. And then Paul, scraping at ash in the folds of his hand, became nostalgic for something, something he couldn't quite pinpoint.

"Did any of it actually happen, Raymond?" he asked.

"Any of what?"

"Our lives, our stories. I know most of it is bullshit but some of it must be true."

"You're right," Raymond agreed, "a lot of it is bull-shit. But a lot of it isn't. Let me put it this way, every-thing that happened last night—the fire, the explosion, the night spent in the cabin—all of that wouldn't even make the top ten of our finest adventures."

"Sounds like a book worth reading."

"Indeed. How about a shot of something?" Raymond suggested.

"Why? What on earth is there to celebrate?" Paul asked.

"Suffering, what else? All life is suffering—and if you haven't suffered then you haven't lived."

"Who are you now? Albert Camus?"

"Funny you say that, I had a drink with Camus once, in a dingy little absinthe joint on the outskirts of Paris. Lovely guy, if a little odd."

"No you didn't, Raymond," Paul shut him off. "No you didn't."

Raymond stopped talking and stared at his friend. Then he looked away.

"You're right, Paul, I didn't. It was all bullshit, wasn't it?" Paul nodded and returned to his coffee.

22

Paul walked through what remained of the villa. He ran a finger along what used to be his kitchen bench, now badly charred and lit up by the sun in the absence of a roof. It crumbled away under his touch. He walked through the frame of what had been the doorway to the bedroom and looked at the bed he'd once shared with Samia. Under the singed springs of the mattress embers still burnt. Everything was black, everything was charcoal. In the living room, which was spared the worst of the explosion, he was surprised to see a small pile of books had survived. One of which was the diary he'd bought in Paris. He flicked through its blank pages to his second entry, his last entry. It read:

There was an explosion. Then nothing. What explosion is strong enough to destroy a world?

Well, he thought, as he closed the diary and tossed it into a pile of ash, now there'd been another explosion.

Another world destroyed. Too bad. He was cursed, he decided, first he'd lost Rebecca, then Vanessa and now this, but Paul didn't know why he'd been cursed. Paul was a good man, mostly, but like all good men he'd done bad things. He'd done plenty of bad things, he knew this because he remembered them all. How could he forget them? On very dark nights Paul would play them back in his mind's eye like snippets of scenes out of films. They haunted him, these twisted memories. They would never leave him in peace. They were violent memories. Sexual. Angry. Secret. Perverse. No dark thoughts on dark nights, he'd say to himself. But then they'd overwhelm him and he'd drown in the well of self-loathing.

Unlike Raymond, Paul didn't like to talk about his past. Where as Raymond would embellish it, Paul would diminish it, and then change the conversation. The past was to be feared, to be reviled and kept under lock and key. But he had mostly been good, hadn't he? Why then the curse? Maybe, actually, Paul had mostly been a bad man. Who could say, there was no-one except Raymond left from those days, and every word from Raymond's mouth was bullshit.

Paul left the villa and walked through the space where the garden had once been. It was nothing but black earth and smoking stumps. All the hard work Samia had done, all the hard work they all had done, for nothing. He went to the poplar, horizontal to the earth, which had once saved his life. It was gone too, just the burnt out trunk remained. To his left the headland looked mostly ok, he could just see the cabin on the beach and decided to walk towards it. The path was still discernible amongst the carnage and he walked along it for as long as he could.

As he approached the sand he removed his shoes and felt the wetness between his toes. It felt so good that he stripped down to nothing and waded into the water.

In the sea he found peace at last. Water was life, rebirth, redemption. He floated on his back and remembered Samia, what it was like to touch her, to taste her, to be inside her. It'd been two weeks since the fire, and he hadn't spoken to her once. One evening she'd come down from her room above the cafe to find Paul at the bar, alone.

"Hi," Samia had said, "are you doing ok?"

He said nothing to her in reply. He just stared at his own reflection in the greasy back-bar mirror and finished his beer in a single sip. Then he stood up and brushed past her and went up to his room. As he went up the stairs he could hear her begin to cry. He paused at the top step, listening to her weeping, and wanted to turn around and hug her. He wanted to hold her and kiss her and brush away any strands of hair caught in her eyelashes. But he didn't, instead he carried on to his room, curled up on his bed and tried to sleep. He remained like that for three days.

Samia had done nothing wrong, of course not. In fact she'd probably saved his life, but Paul was unable to bring himself to talk to her. On one hand he felt as if they'd betrayed his daughter by making love, that they'd tarnished her memory somehow. Was it perverse for him to love the same flesh his daughter once had? But his daughter was gone. If Paul didn't make love to Samia then someone else would and that someone else might treat her badly. Surely Vanessa would have wanted Paul and Samia to be together, right? Probably not, he decided, actually, no, of course not. How could she?

At the same time he'd exploited Samia's vulnerability, he'd diminished her. He'd taken something pure, her love for his daughter, and turned it into something toxic, his lust for her flesh. But he didn't lust for her flesh, he never had. He connected with her over something deeper, over the countless little intricacies of shared grief which no one else could ever understand. Grief had bonded them, in a way neither could have expected. He'd hurt Vanessa, maybe, but she was dead, and Samia was not. He wanted Samia again, he wanted to never let her go, to never take his lips off hers. This internal conflict had filled his mind with a thousand and one questions he could never know the answers to. It had left him rattled. But out in the sea, he couldn't not think of her. He had, after all, admitted to Raymond that he loved her, hadn't he? And what was love, if not overwhelming when alone in the sea?

After the swim he dried himself in the sun and began the walk back to town. Fifty yards from the villa was the burnt wreck of his motorcycle, it'd been tossed through the sky like a frisbee when the truck had exploded. It was a fine bike, it had served its purpose for a while, but he wasn't particularly fussed about its loss. Besides, he was happy to be without it for the walk into town was long and he had a lot to think about. A lot to mull over, decisions had to be made.

That evening there was to be a gala to raise money for the regeneration of the wilderness destroyed in the fire. It was for a good cause, as the wilderness was unique and home to several endemic species, not least of all the playful little turtles Paul had a special fondness for. But

Paul wasn't quite ready for a gala, he wasn't quite ready for small talk and endless pity and fake charm. He knew Raymond was going, and Samia too, and he didn't know if he was ready to see them either. Raymond had been badgering him about it all week, and he knew he'd be at it again this evening.

As he walked towards the village he took a shortcut through a vineyard and began to feel lethargic in the unguarded glare of the sun. He laid down to rest in the warmth of the gentle afternoon. After a short while he drifted off to sleep, and returned to his same recurring dream, on the harbour back in Sydney with his daughter, Vanessa.

She is radiant, full of hope and expectations and anxieties about being away from her father. He reassures her she'll be fine, her French is improving every day and her nature alone will ensure she'll never be lonely. If anyone can charm a room it is his daughter. The dream always starts out like this, pleasant and soothing on the bobbing tide, his arm around her and her head nestled into him as the ferry drifts through the shaded water under the bridge. And then it turns dark. Suddenly Paul notices smoke coming from the engine room and he stands up to investigate. As he does so the hatch kicks open and out of the flames staggers Raymond, his index finger prodding Paul in the chest.

"Tell her what you've done, Paul, tell her everything."

Paul pushes Raymond back into the fire and his friend cries out in pain as he vanishes into the flames. He rushes back to Vanessa and wraps his arms around her but she pushes him away.

"You have betrayed me," she says, her eyes fierce and

fixed to his own. "You have betrayed me," she repeats.

Suddenly the boat begins to rock and Paul is thrust overboard. He cries out for her hand as she just stands there and watches him drown. Then, just before he goes under and is lost for good, she reaches out towards him and starts shaking him.

Suddenly, Paul woke up and was shocked to find a figure standing over him. The dream vanished just as quickly as it had appeared. It took a moment for his eyes to adjust before he realised it was Achille.

"I've been looking for you, Paul," he said in his mumbled version of French. Then he reached out a hand and pulled Paul to his feet.

"You have, why's that?" Paul asked, only half awake and feeling groggy on his legs.

"Denise was worried you might have jumped this time. Right off the cliff. I've been down at the base searching for your remains."

"It hadn't even occurred to me," Paul replied, confused. "I just went through the wreckage and had a swim. What right does she have?"

"Don't take it personally," Achille reassured him, "it's not about you, Paul, it's about her. There's nothing that woman loves more than the idea of suicide. To this day she still resents me for not having done it yet. She's read too many damn books."

As the two men climbed into Achille's truck and drove back into town, Paul remained quiet, not bothering to try to understand what Achille had just told him.

23

Samia had been opposed to the idea of attending the gala at first, but as always, she found Raymond's charm irresistible and came around to it.

"Come," he begged her, "you can be my date. I've never had a woman with even one-tenth of your elegance on my arm."

She laughed.

"But what about Paul? I feel bad just leaving him alone."

"What difference does it make? You come with me and Paul will wallow in his misery, you stay at the cafe and he will do same. The man is broken, forget about him."

"You're sure he won't come?" she asked, ignoring his last remark.

"I doubt it, but it'd be good for him if he did. If he doesn't break out of his rut soon you can bet your last nickel we'll lose him for good."

While Paul had been at the villa sorting through

the wreckage and swimming in the sea, Raymond and Samia had driven down to Cavalaire to bask in the sunshine and stroll along the promenade. It was a lovely day, with a misty blue sky and a tender sun that kept them warm against the incessant ocean breeze. It was hard to believe the same landscape had produced the horrors of two weeks ago, the disaster on the cape. Samia stopped and faced the sea, then she turned to Raymond who stood solemnly beside her.

"Do you think he hates me?" she asked.

"Of course he doesn't hate you, a man would sooner hate his own reflection than the likes of you."

"I'm being serious, Raymond. We slept together. You know right? Or didn't he tell you?"

Raymond shook his head. "He didn't say a damn thing, but I assumed as much. Only Paul could be so stupid."

"Why is that stupid?" Samia asked, surprised to find herself so defensive.

"Because what good could come of it? Your life is in Paris and his life is anywhere but there, he said so himself. On top of that it's more complicated, isn't it?"

"It is," she said as she sat on the rocky seawall, her legs dangling over the edge. "I loved his daughter too, before him, she was magnificent. It's very complicated. And stupid, you're right."

"So, you do love him?"

Samia shook her head and said nothing for a moment while she gathered her thoughts.

"No, I don't. But he is very kind to me, or he was kind to me, and now he is acting like a bastard. But he has hurt so much so I can't blame him for it."

"Paul was always complicated, ever since I've known

him there's been a conflict inside of him. As a young man Paul was in and out of jail, I bet he never told you that."

"No, he didn't. What'd he do?"

"Nothing terrible, just petty crimes. Break and enter, stealing cars and all that crap. Somewhere along the line he came across a camera and it forced him to sort his shit out before it was too late. And luckily, for everyone, he did."

This surprised Samia, for Paul had seemed a gentle man, an honest man. But she thought about her friends in Paris, many of them gentle and honest too, and several of them had been lured to the wrong side of the law. She herself had never been like that, although since the attacks in Paris she'd copped plenty of racial abuse which had made her want to break out, hurt something or someone or usually just herself.

"I hope he's ok," she said.

"I'm sure he'll be fine, now let's go," Raymond urged her, "we'll head over to my place and get ready for to-night. I have some outfits from previous wives you might fit into."

"It seems an odd time to party," she admitted, "what is there to possibly celebrate?"

"Once we're there you'll be fine. I have a lot of inter-esting friends I'll introduce you to. It'll take your mind off things."

Samia looked up to him and smiled as he reached out his hand and helped her to her feet.

"You're a good friend, Raymond," she said.

"It's been a long time since anyone's said that," the old man reminisced. "Thank you."

The gala was on the lawn of a winery at La Croix Valmer. Everyone with deep pockets from Marseille all the way to Nice had been invited, and the early evening stars sparkled with an elegance that rivalled the guest's outfits. Samia had chosen a sleek black dress left over from Raymond's fourth wife and short black heels left over from his fifth. She didn't normally dress like this, in fact she couldn't remember a single time when she had, and she found walking on the gravel and the turf awkward in the heels. She looked as awkward as a racehorse walking over cobblestones. Raymond wore a brown dinner jacket over a white linen shirt and black trousers. Samia had helped him groom his beard and as she stroked his face she noticed for the first time just how attractive she found him. If he looked this good at 78, he must have been a real catch when he was younger, she thought. She found it strange that he never spoke of his friends or lovers or even family, he only ever made offhand jokes about his ex-wives. What had this man done to turn everyone in his life so against him? She was spellbound by him, she'd only ever been able to see his charm, what was she missing?

The chateau attached to the lawn was marvellous, with enormous roman pillars carved out of sandstone and elegant balconies draped with bougainvilleas. It was like a dream to Samia, she'd never known such elegance, and Raymond smiled as he watched her introduce herself to the other guests.

"You were there, weren't you," asked Jonas Selinofoto, a Greek shipping tycoon who had a holiday house not far from Raymond's home.

"I was," Samia said, as Raymond passed her a flute

of champagne, "it was hellish. I thought for sure we were both going to die."

"Luckily this man was here to save you," Jonas joked, elbowing Raymond in the ribs.

"Actually, yes, we were lucky, my friend Paul had gone mad with fear. I couldn't control him on my own."

"Paul was the one who owned the villa, correct?" Jonas asked.

"Yes, it's a sad story."

"It doesn't have to be," Jonas suggested, "he can rebuild again, that land won't burn like that for at least a decade. And let's be honest, that villa was from another time, it needed to be demolished for something more modern. Every time I'd drive past I'd wonder how it could possibly still be standing."

"I suppose so, but I liked it there. Plus it was named after his daughter, who is dead."

Jonas gave her a conciliatory look and rested a hand on her shoulder.

"Speaking of daughters, where's mine?" he asked.

"I saw her by the band," Raymond said. "Come Samia, you need to meet her. She's probably the only other person here remotely close to your age."

Katerina Selinofoto was a young woman with the world at her feet. She was vibrant and alluring, with sun-bleached blonde hair and hazel eyes which, on clear nights, reflected the moonlight as if they were jewels. She was already wealthy and famous, ranked 20th in the world for women's tennis. She'd just reached the quarter finals of the French Open for the first time and had travelled to the south of France to stay with her father at his holiday home in Gassin, hoping for some well earned rest and relaxation.

When Samia saw her, standing by the three piece band playing Spanish instrumentals, she was immediately thankful that Raymond had convinced her to attend that evening. Samia didn't believe in love at first sight, but lust at first sight? Well she believed in that, definitely.

"Katerina," Jonas called across the small audience gathered by the music, "come over here."

Katerina turned and smiled at her father, and then excused herself from the company of the older women who'd crowded her with praise for her performance at the Open.

"This is Samia, from Paris, she's been holidaying down here too, but the villa she was living in was destroyed in the fire," Jonas said.

"I'm so sorry," Katerina offered her condolences.

"Don't be," Samia replied, "as your father said the villa had had its time, it meant nothing."

Katerina smiled, then she apologised again. "Also I'm sorry I don't speak any French, although I know I should learn."

"It's ok," Samia reassured her, "I don't speak any Greek at all so it's me who should be sorry."

"But we're not in Greece, this is your country."

"I wish we were in Greece," Samia said, "I imagine it's very beautiful there."

"It is," Katerina exclaimed, "it's the most beautiful place in the world. If we become friends you could visit me there one day. I live on an island named Hydra, there's not much to do there but swim in the sea all day and relax with wine in the evening."

"It sounds like a dream," Samia mused.

"Then you must visit me," Katerina pleaded as she reached out and stroked Samia's arm. "Come, let's get another drink."

Samia turned and blushed at Raymond as Katerina led her away towards the bar.

"Looks like the girls have hit it off," Jonas said.

"More than you know," Raymond chuckled. "Now how about you and I? Who here is single?"

"Let's find out," Jonas laughed, as he followed his friend away from the band.

From his room above the cafe Paul could hear the music of the gala, and he wrestled with the temptation to head down and take a look. He knew Samia would be there. There was no way Raymond would allow her to stay home and wallow in her pity. He knew this because Raymond had tried just about everything that week to convince Paul to attend, and Samia was much more genial than him.

"Fine," he muttered, as he thrust his legs off his bed and faced himself in the mirror. "I'll go for a bit, apologise to Samia and return home in an hour. What harm can come of it?"

He got up and started to flick through some clothes Raymond had brought over for him. He tried on a suede jacket and some blue jeans and thought he looked quite handsome. He hadn't shaved in many days, and the silver stubble gave him the air of an adventurer, like he used to be in his glory days as a photographer. He slipped on some shoes and said goodnight to Denise as he raced out the door and down towards the vineyard. He felt good now, in control. He played out the scenarios in his head. He'd walk down the driveway, enter the chateau and find the bar. He'd order a scotch and lean against a wall as he browsed the room. Then Samia would see him, and she'd look dazzling. She'd walk over to him, slowly, and compliment him on his outfit. And then he'd kiss her.

As he approached the gala he took a deep breath and pulled a mint out of his pocket. Then he entered the chateau and searched for a face he recognised in the crowd, but he couldn't see one. He ordered a scotch at the bar and continued to drift through the crowd while searching for her. Having no luck he decided to head to the bathroom and see if she might be waiting in line. As he moved through the corridors he fiddled with his outfit, adjusting his jacket and arranging his hair. And then he saw her.

Samia was pressed against a wall in a dimly lit corridor just before the female toilets, while another woman, an even younger woman, with sun-bleached blonde hair and hazel eyes, pressed herself up against her. Their lips were locked together as their hands explored the other's body with feverish abandon. Paul watched for a moment, and went to say something, but decided not to. He raised his drink to his lips and finished the whole thing, then turned away and left the two young women in peace.

24

The next morning Paul woke up in Raymond's living room. He realised this when he found the strength to sit upright and finally open his eyes. From the balcony streams of light tormented him, and the damned rhinoceros's head, high above the fireplace, judged him with stoic eyes. Inside his skull a throbbing pain rendered him all but useless. What had happened last night? What had he done this time? Did he manage to fuck everything up again? He feared the worst. He reached around for a glass of water, but this time he was let down—there wasn't one. As he managed to stand up, Raymond entered the room. His energy was bright and vivacious, as it always was after a night spent drinking, the complete opposite of Paul's.

"How you feeling?" Raymond asked, as he handed his friend some pain medication and glass of water. Paul devoured both before answering.

"How do you think?" he responded, wiping his mouth dry with the sleeve of his shirt.

"I wouldn't know Paul, I don't pop pills."

"Pop pills?" Paul asked, indignant.

"That's right, you and Susana were having a good old time swallowing whatever garbage she could fish from her purse. Until her husband turned up and sorted things out quick smart."

"Susana?" Paul mumbled. "Her husband?"

"So you remember none of it then?"

"No, nothing. Well, I remember something," Paul stammered, as the image of Samia and her lover pressed against the wall returned to him. He felt a fire rise in his stomach, but his head was in too much pain to bother dealing with it. "Why am I here, Raymond?" Paul continued. "Why aren't I in my room?"

"Come, let me get you a coffee and I'll explain it all in the garden."

By the time Raymond had prepared the coffee and dusted off the outdoor furniture, Paul's headache had subsided enough for him to navigate a conversation. They sat overlooking the view towards the sea, and Paul thought he could make out Cap Lardier through the haze of the rising heat. It brought back memories of Samia and the villa, and he felt a dagger twist in his gut.

"Thanks Raymond, I really need this right now," Paul said as he reached for his mug.

"I can never start the day without a coffee," Raymond agreed. "The only problem is the French have no clue how to make them."

"I'm not talking about the coffee, Raymond, I'm talking about the company."

Raymond shifted a little uneasily in his chair, he wasn't used to Paul being so sentimental, so earnest. Their friendship was a pained one, mostly due to Raymond's tryst with Paul's long dead wife, but also because their energies never quite aligned. Raymond's flamboyance didn't sit right with Paul, and Paul's demure indifference bored Raymond. It were as if there was a wall between them, which had stopped them from ever really connecting on some kind of deeper level. Sure, there'd been emergencies, orgies, red carpets and plane crashes they'd survived together. They'd seen each other nude too many times to count, had enough gossip on the other to get them arrested and had, under moonless nights adrift in the Sahara, shared their deepest, darkest fears with the other. But something had always been amiss. Still, they endured one another, for everyone else had abandoned them both.

"Did I fuck up?" Paul asked, his eyes fixed to the cape.

"Not as bad as you could have."

"And what the hell does that mean?" he asked, bitterly.

"It means you didn't hurt Samia, and that's all that matters right now."

"Did I try?" Paul pried.

"You thought about it, sure. You're Paul Greene, aren't you? Of course you tried."

"What happened?"

"I didn't let you, you can thank me later," Raymond grinned.

"I saw her with someone."

"That's not your business, Paul."

"It could have been."

"Maybe, but it isn't," Raymond said sternly, putting the matter to rest.

"You're right, that doesn't explain why I'm here though."

"You're here because you had no where else to go."

"I have a hotel room?"

"You lost the keys."

"I did? Shit."

"It's ok, I spoke to Denise this morning, she has a spare set waiting for you. After you stormed off from the party I found you passed out in front of the cafe. You were a miserable sight, covered in your own spew, your limbs sprawled out in the street with the gutter acting as a pillow. You're lucky I found you before you were run over."

Paul was silent for a few moments as he visualised everything his friend had just said.

"I'm sorry Raymond, they were your clothes."

"Forget about it, the maid is on it already."

"What happened with Susana?" Paul asked.

"Well," Raymond started, "if you remember what I told you, which I doubt you do, her and her husband like to maintain appearances. When you started going at her-"

"Going at her?" Paul interrupted.

"Yeah going at her, screwing her in the vineyard in plain view of the party. Well, her husband took exception to it."

"That's why my jaw feels like it's broken in three places?" Paul asked as he rubbed at his chin.

"Possibly, there's a few reasons for that."

"Did Samia see?"

"Everything," Raymond nodded.

"I need to talk to her."

"I wouldn't Paul, she was pretty shaken. Give her a day or two. Or maybe a week or two."

"No, Raymond," Paul ignored his advice, "I need to

talk to her today. I'll return to the cafe and apologise to whoever I have to and then I'll knock on Samia's door and apologise for everything. It's the least I can do."

"Well, you won't have any luck I'm sorry."

"What do you mean?"

"She isn't staying at the cafe any longer."

"She's returned to Paris?" Paul asked, his heart suddenly racing.

"No. She's staying with my friend Jonas, not far from here. I think she's taken a liking to his daughter."

So that was the girl, Raymond's friend's daughter, and Raymond had introduced them, Paul figured. Of course he had, he was always trying to interfere with the women in Paul's life. The miserable bastard had already tried to ruin one of his relationships, and now he had to dig his fingers into this. Paul got to his feet and looked down at his old friend.

"Where does Jonas live, Raymond?" he asked.

"I'm not going to tell you, Paul."

"Tell me, Raymond," he shouted.

"My lips are sealed," Raymond shrugged, turning away.

"Raymond, tell me now or I swear this friendship is over," Paul demanded.

Raymond chuckled, and reached for his pipe which he began to pack with tobacco.

"This friendship's been over, Paul," he mused, smiling up at him, silhouetted by the midday sun, "ever since the night I fucked your wife."

Paul wanted to kill him, he wanted to strangle the life out of him, but instead he just kicked over his chair and limped away, having hurt his foot in the process.

When he got to the gate at the end of Raymond's driveway he was unable to open it, so he scaled the fence
beside it and fell in a heap on the other side.

Raymond Bishop, the lothario who'd dishonoured
the love of his life, the narcissist who'd ignored his grief
over his lost daughter, the puppet master who'd stolen
Samia from him, was as good as dead to Paul. As Paul
staggered down the hill away from Raymond's estate,
he cursed the day he'd arrived back in France.

Fuck this country, he thought to himself, it couldn't
protect Vanessa and it's done nothing to save me.

Paul's plan became clear in his head, he'd return to
his hotel, he'd shower and pack what little he had left.
Then he'd get the bus to Toulon and the train to Marseille. From Marseille he'd catch a flight out of France,
somewhere like Greece, he decided, where his money
could stretch a little further, and he'd die out his days
living off booze in a little shack by the sea. Fuck the rest,
he thought, the rest never did me any good. I should
have stuck to crime.

As he rounded the bend the village came into view.
He walked the final few kilometres with great difficulty
as cars slowed beside him, to either stare or offer help,
bemused by his limp. He ignored them all. When he
finally reached the town and then the cafe he noticed
a strange look on Denise's face. She was about to say
something when Achille silenced her with a gesture.
Paul staggered over to the bar and asked for a key.

"Here you are, Mr Greene," she said cautiously as
she handed one to him. "Do you need me to do anything for you?"

"Nothing at all," Paul replied, "I got it all worked out

up here," he said as he pressed a finger against his skull.

Paul hobbled up the stairs, for the first time in his life having to rely on a hand rail, and unlocked the door to his room.

He didn't know what he expected to see when he opened it, but he knew he didn't expect to see her sitting on the edge of his bed, alone. Her eyes fixed on him.

"Are you ok?" Samia asked.

"Are you?" he responded.

25

Paul closed the door behind him and sat at the chair by the small writing desk. He lifted his leg and turned his ankle clockwise and then anti clockwise, it hurt like hell.

"Want me to look at it?" Samia asked, rising to her feet.

"No, it's fine, it's just twisted."

"Here," she said as she knelt by him and removed his shoe, "don't be so stubborn and let me take a look."

Paul winced with pain as she slid the shoe off and removed the sock. Samia inspected it, the ankle was badly swollen and there was an abrasion on the inside of the foot.

"Wait a moment," she instructed him, "please, don't move. I'll be quick."

Samia left the room and went down to the bar to get some ice from Denise.

"How is he?" Denise asked as she scooped some out from the ice-well.

"He isn't good. He's had a rough time since the fire, I worry about him. I want to be angry at him, because I deserve to be angry at him, but I just pity him. Whenever I see him now I wonder if it'll be the last time."

"Take care of him, darling, he is a good man."

Samia returned to Paul and applied the ice to his ankle. With her thumb and forefinger she massaged the bridge of his foot until the pain became unbearable and he pulled away. She looked up at him, his clothes were matted with dirt and weeds and he had a sequence of small cuts up his arm like rungs on a ladder. There was an abrasion on his jaw, from the punch she'd witnessed.

"What on earth has happened to you, Paul?" she asked, her concern obvious in her eyes.

"I have no idea, I ran into some bad company I guess," he said.

"How do you know you weren't the bad company?"

"You're right, of course, I'm always the bad guy."

"You're not bad Paul, just stupid," she tried to joke.

"I take it that's a compliment?"

"Yes, and it's the only one I'll be giving. Now, let me look at your arm."

With a damp cloth from the bathroom Samia cleaned the cuts on his arm and applied some antiseptic cream she found in a first-aid kit under the sink.

"You're too old to be running around like a madman, Mr. Greene," she smiled as she applied the cream. "Do we have to put you in a home where you can be supervised?"

"You're not funny, Samia, how would you like it if I offered to check you into a kindergarten?"

"I wish it were possible, life was much more simple then, wasn't it."

Once she was satisfied that Paul had been cared for

as well as possible, she returned to the edge of the bed and stared at him.

"Anything you want to say?" she asked.

"Yes, there is," he muttered.

"Well, go on."

"Why do we still never talk about Vanessa?"

Samia remained quiet a moment, taken aback by his response. It wasn't what she'd expected.

"You know, I was thinking maybe a thank you or a sorry, but sure, why not, let's talk about Vanessa."

"What's it like to lose a lover?" Paul asked.

"Haven't you also lost a lover?"

"I lost a soulmate, that's different. Very different. I want to understand your experience."

"Well, what if she was my soulmate too? What if her and I were destined to go on forever?"

"Then tell me about it," he demanded, losing his cool.

"It fucking hurt, ok? It hurt like fucking hell," Samia said as she resisted the urge to break down and cry. "I stopped eating, I stopped getting out of bed in the morning. I hated everyone around me, especially my cousins who thought the whole thing was a joke. Vanessa and I were bullied for being together, for being gay. Can you imagine how much worse that was when she wasn't beside me any longer? How hard it was not having her with me to tell them to fuck off? I missed her touch, her smell, her jokes. I didn't touch another person until you, Paul. Did you know that? I went from daughter to father without missing a beat. Don't tell me soulmates are different, because if Vanessa wasn't my soulmate then nobody will ever be."

Paul said nothing, he didn't know what to say. He

never knew what to say. Eventually she broke the silence.

"And you? You lost a daughter, right? What's that like?" she asked, composing herself.

Paul looked at her, his expression unreadable.

"When you have a child, you stop living for yourself. Especially if it is a good child, like Vanessa, a special one. You live for her and her only. Every morning when the alarm goes off, and you pull yourself out of bed and drag yourself to the shower you're doing it for her. The long weeks on assignments, the assholes above you and the idiots under you, you tolerate all of them for her. You feed her, clothe her, protect her. Every little moment of your day is about her. Over time you stop existing, in the way you used to exist, at least. That person, the person you used to be, isn't relevant, that person doesn't matter anymore. Just her. Then someone takes her away from you, kills her needlessly and violently. And then when the alarm goes off you can't get out of bed, what's the point? You begin telling those above you and under you to fuck off. There's nothing to lose now, is there? You've already lost everything. You stopped existing so that she could, then when she stops existing and you still do you are left with nothing. You become a ghost, a phantom, and you quickly realise the sooner it all just ends the better off everyone would be. You need to disappear, the world demands it of you. And so you do. You find a little known corner of the world and you wear the invisible cloak and you wait silently for that final breath to set you free."

He turned and looked at her, a tear caressed his cheek.

"You shouldn't have saved me from the fire, Samia," he continued. "You should have left me there to burn."

"No Paul," she said as she crossed the room and kneeled before him. "You still have a lot to give."

"I have nothing Samia. I am nothing. The world is cruel and there's no point trying to fool yourself otherwise. The sooner you learn that lesson the better off you'll be, now please, leave me."

"No," she whispered.

"Get out of my room!" he shouted.

"I won't leave you, not tonight," she sobbed.

"Why?"

"I don't trust you."

"What?"

"I don't trust you not to hurt yourself."

"You didn't listen to anything. Get out!" he shouted again.

"Please Paul, let me stay with you."

"Won't you be missed?"

"What do you mean?"

"I saw you last night, pressed up against the wall with another woman. Won't she be missing you?"

"That's entirely irrelevant Paul," she defended herself.

"You move fast, girl."

"What does that mean?"

"Vanessa, myself, whoever that woman was. Without missing a beat, as you said. Fast!"

"Fuck you," she spat, moving away from him.

"You already did, and it meant nothing."

"Yes it did, Paul."

"Bullshit."

"You said yourself it was wrong, you said yourself we couldn't continue. Don't put this on me."

"Leave Samia, leave and don't look back."

"Raymond was right."

"Excuse me?"

"He said you were an asshole. He warned me not to get too close."

"Funny that, he'd know a thing or two. Why don't you go ask Raymond why he's been through six wives? I doubt you'd have him on such a pedestal then."

"Be quiet Paul. Put yourself down, but not the rest of us."

"Get out!" he cried, loud enough for Denise and Achille to hear downstairs.

"I thought you were better than this."

"Well I'm telling you I'm fucking not. Now leave."

"Vanessa would be so ashamed."

"You barely knew my daughter for longer than a minute. Don't pretend you meant anything to her."

"Good bye Paul."

"Get out and stay out."

After Samia left, Paul sat silent for an hour, then did exactly what he'd promised himself he would, he packed what little had left and checked out of the hotel. Denise was devastated.

"Mr. Greene," she begged, "please don't rush out like this."

He ignored her and threw his keys on the bar top.

"Things never end well," Denise continued, "when a man listens to the fire in his belly. Stay, have a drink, think it over. There's no reason to run," she pleaded.

"There's no reason not to run, either," Paul said as he turned away from her and left.

Denise walked over to where Achille sat, who had silently watched the exchange. She imagined Paul's obituary, how literary it would read, how exciting it would be, and she felt a pang of guilt when she realised she was looking forward to reading it.

The journey to Marseille was uneventful, apart from a heaviness in Paul's heart, which tried to tug him back to Samia. He ignored it and did his best to sleep. In Marseille he headed straight to the airport and looked at the flight schedule, there was one to Tangiers in just under three hours. Paul had visited Tangiers when he was younger. He remembered a colonial style hotel on the cliffs which was full of broken men, and figured it was as good as any other place in the world to disappear in.

I'd just be joining a long list, he thought, a long list of other hapless fools who've vanished in the casbah of Tangiers, never to be seen again.

He arrived just before midday and made his way to the Hotel Continental, an enormous 19th century building nestled into yellowing cliffs and overlooking the harbour. The man at the desk welcomed him with a smile, partially hidden under a grey moustache, and greeted Paul in English.

"Welcome to the Hotel Continental, sir. May I know the name of the booking?" he asked.

"I don't have a booking," Paul responded. "Is that going to be a problem?"

"Of course not," the man reassured him, "we always keep a few rooms empty for the lost souls who float in with the tide."

"Sure, whatever," Paul grumbled. "I'll need it for a month, maybe more, it's impossible to know."

"Certainly," the man said, as he typed away at his antiquated computer. "You're in room 223, second floor.

Anything else I can help you with?" the man asked as he handed Paul the key.

"Yeah, there is actually. I need something to smoke, is there a way I can get something through you guys, or should I head to the medina?"

The cashier gave Paul a knowing smile. "I'll send someone up shortly, Mr. Greene."

"Thank you," Paul said, and then he went to his room for some much needed solitude.

26

Samia had not seemed herself, Raymond thought. Even the presence of Katerina, her glorious fling who fawned over her, was not enough to pull her from her rut. Ever since that argument with Paul a week earlier, Samia had been deeply depressed. Paul had vanished, leaving no apparent clue as to where he might have gone, and Samia acted as if she didn't care. But deep down she worried for him, of course she did, he was like a boy with a thousand broken hearts. Paul was capable of anything, Denise had warned her, and it'd be unlikely any of them would ever see him again. Life had weighed heavily on her ever since.

One afternoon, in an effort to lighten Samia's mood, Raymond invited Jonas and Katerina over for lunch in his garden, where they could bask in the breath of the wild jasmine that shaded his porch. He organised a caterer and set them up at the same table where he'd last sat and spoken with Paul, before Paul ran off like a madman into the setting sun.

As Jonas uncorked a bottle of local white wine he'd purchased at the market that very morning, and Katerina stretched out over Samia in the dappled sunlight, he proposed a trip.

"We charter a yacht," Jonas started, "and the four of us sail to my island home—Hydra. We can do it over a week or two. We have a villa there, nestled in the cliffs and protected from the wind. And the best part is we can stay there as long as we please, until either Katerina returns to training or Samia returns to her studies. Or we all tire of one another."

"And what about me?" Raymond asked.

"You? What must you return to?" Jonas joked.

"Nothing," Raymond conceded, lighting his pipe, "absolutely nothing at all. In fact I'd be a wise man to die out there."

"A man has to die somewhere," Jonas teased, his oversized waist jiggling as he laughed, "it may as well be on a Greek island with a view of the Aegean."

Without any warning Samia shoved Katerina's legs off her and stood up, excusing herself from the table.

"All this talk of dying lately has tired me," she said. "First Denise tells me that Paul is as good as dead, probably by his own hand, and now Raymond won't stop talking about his own death. Have you all forgotten why I am here? Or is it that you don't care?"

Raymond opened his mouth to apologise but Samia stormed away before he could find the right words. Katerina turned to her father who suggested she give Samia a moment to herself. So she did, and the three of them did their best to enjoy the lunch. Later that afternoon, Katerina found Samia on a rocking chair on the balcony, just as the sun began to set.

"Are you ok?" Katerina asked as she knelt down in front of her, her fingers stroking the backs of her calves.

"I'm fine," Samia shrugged, her eyes fixed to the shimmering horizon.

"We don't have to go on the boat," Katerina reassured her lover, "we can stay here if that's what you'd prefer."

"No, I want to, I really do. I want to see where you're from, I want to hear you speak your own language," Samia smiled. "In the evenings we can cook Greek food and sing Greek songs and drink ouzo and then swim together in the sea when the night is almost dead."

"Can we swim nude?" Katerina teased.

"Always," she smiled, and then kissed her, "clothes will be illegal when the two of us are together. I need to leave here," she said, shifting the conversation away from playful, "it's been a struggle for me, ever since I've arrived. It's felt as if I'm in a boxing match with an endless number of rounds. The blows just keep knocking me down."

"Well they finish today, ok. My father has been on the phone all afternoon and there is a yacht we can take tomorrow, just the four of us and two crew. If you like we can sail away from here and never return."

"There is nothing for me here," Samia agreed, "not anymore, anyway."

"Nothing," Katerina repeated.

The two young women remained silent, their hands interlocked, as they watched the afternoon fade into night from the comfort of the balcony. That evening, for the first time in months, Samia slept through the night without waking up to terrifying visions of Vanessa. Instead she woke up to the gentle touch of Katerina, stroking her under the covers with the backs of her finger nails. When they woke the next morning they made love—slow, languid morning love—and showered, got dressed and packed. Then they took a taxi with Jonas and Raymond to the port of Cavailaire where the yacht was waiting.

"Shit," Samia said to Raymond as they climbed aboard, "we didn't say goodbye to Denise or Achille."

"You'll be back kid," Raymond reassured her.

"And what if I never come back?" she asked.

"Well, if something happens to me out there," he said, looking towards the sea, "you'll have no choice but to come back here and sort out my affairs, there's some papers on my desk upstairs I want you to look over."

"You promised me you'd finished talking this nonsense."

"Well I lied to you, now be a sweetheart and take these bags down to the cabin," he said, handing her his luggage, "whichever room looks the best, that one's mine."

They got themselves comfortable onboard and set sail that afternoon just after 1pm. The conditions were perfect, with a decent wind behind them and smooth, sunny seas ahead. Jonas and Katerina, both experienced at sea, helped out the captain and his crew member while Samia and Raymond relaxed on the bow.

"What are you thinking about?" he asked her.

"Nothing really, just life I suppose," she answered.

"And what is it about life that's got you so transfixed?"

"Well, to start with, it's cruel, it's always cruel. Everyone knows this, it's the only one true thing everyone can surely agree on. But when I look out ahead at the sea and the sun I realise that it is very beautiful too."

"And what wins out in the end? The cruelness or the beauty?"

"You tell me, you're the old man," she laughed.

"Well I'll let you in on a secret—neither wins, it's all bullshit. The trick to it is getting through the day. You do that then you've got every chance of getting through the next day. Then the day after that and so on."

"And if you don't?"

"Then you're dead, you lose."

"So it's a competition then?"

"Of course it is, life is nature and nature is struggle. If you don't compete then you're nothing but bird seed."

Samia didn't respond, she just thought about what he'd said but she couldn't agree with him. Samia wasn't competitive, she'd never been competitive, and she survived better than almost everyone else around her. Vanessa had been competitive, Paul too, and look at them now.

"Do you think he's dead?" she asked Raymond, breaking the silent spell of the sea.

"No," he shook his head, "killing yourself takes guts and Paul hasn't had guts for years."

"You're too harsh on him."

"So you'd rather I said he was dead then?"

"Not at all, of course not. I just wish you'd give him a break sometimes."

"Look," Raymond turned to her, his face serious, "Paul is one of the finest men I've ever known, one of the best friends I've ever had, but the man has been broken by too much heartbreak and he's never found a way to heal from it. I hope he breaks out of it somehow, because the Paul I knew twenty years ago was nothing like the Paul you met."

"I thought Paul was very fine," she protested.

"But did you love him?"

"No, I've already told you I didn't."

"Then there's your reason, because in the past everyone who met Paul loved him, me more than anyone."

Suddenly Katerina called from the stern, "Samia, Raymond, there are dolphins trailing us!"

Raymond turned around and gave her a nod, then he struggled to get back to his feet. "We'll finish this conversation later, if you like."

"It's fine," Samia replied as she helped him up, "let's just try and enjoy ourselves."

As the heat of the sun relaxed and the day lost its brilliance, Jonas sat down with his three companions on the deck and explained the path of their journey over a bottle of champagne.

"We'll stop here," he said, zooming in on his phone with two fingers over a map of the Mediterranean, "in a town named Calvi. We'll spend two days there before setting sail around the west coast of Corsica and then through the straits above Sardinia. We'll head down to Porto-Vecchio, then we'll head straight to Naples. After a night or two there we'll charge south and skirt around Sicily, then we'll cross the Ionian and make the last leg in a day or two. Any questions?"

"How long all up?" Raymond asked, as he began to pack his pipe against the wind.

"Well," Jonas paused, "we can do it as quickly or as slowly as you'd like. If we treat it like a sprint we could be there in six days, not bothering to rest along the way. But if we agree to take it slowly we could do it over two or three weeks. I don't think any of us are in a particular hurry, although Katerina you need to stay fit."

It was true, none of them were in a hurry, but deep down Samia felt something tugging at her, something yanking at her soul. Despite her chat with Raymond, she couldn't help but feel that Paul was in trouble, that he needed her or Raymond or both of them, and wherever he was, he was likely hurting himself. She'd seen how Paul was when she'd first arrived at the villa, he was frail and reckless and somehow broken. Exactly how you'd imagine a man who'd lost his only child in a terrorist attack to be. But what of him now, months later, after everything that had happened, everything that had gone wrong? Had she betrayed Paul? If something were to happen to him, were she to blame?

"Are you ok?" Katerina asked as she stroked Samia's back against the cold.

"I'm fine," Samia said, turning away from her to hide. "I'm just overwhelmed," she continued.

"By what?" Katerina asked, concerned.

Samia turned to her lover and composed herself as best she could. "It's nothing serious," she lied, "it's just the beauty of this place, it's so lovely out here, and it makes me want to cry," she said. And then she broke down into tears.

27

Raymond Bishop's final day alive was remarkable. He woke before any of his fellow travellers, the crew included, and fished around in the hull as silently as possible for a snorkel and a pair of goggles. As the others had partied the night before to celebrate their arrival into Calvi, Raymond chose instead to retire to bed around 7pm, while they were still far out at sea. His back had been causing him incessant pain all week, and he'd developed an excruciating cramp inside his gut which he'd been doing his best to keep to himself. But it had become overwhelming so he'd gone to bed. For his entire life, Raymond's way of dealing with medical ailments was to just wait them out, hope they'd go away, and auspiciously they mostly had. But this one hadn't—not yet, and probably not ever.

To hell with it, he thought, there's no chance I'm going out like one of those sons of bitches in hospital, shitting and pissing where they sleep while young docile nurses clench their nostrils and gag as they wipe them clean.

If this was finally cancer, which he was almost certain it was, then he'd let it take him swiftly and if necessary, painfully. But there'd be no operations, no drips, no chemotherapy. Raymond had nothing more to live for. If he had children he'd never met them, and if he had friends they'd all given up on him by now anyway. No, let it come, he willed it on, let the cancer spread and end this farce once and for all. Spread, he willed it, spread you bastard.

Raymond climbed out of the hull, goggles and snorkel in hand, and was immediately taken aback by the beauty of the view that greeted him. He'd never been to Calvi, he'd never even seen a photo of it, but old comrades of his had been there and they'd spoken of it highly. But their words hadn't done it justice.

The sea sparkled like glitter across a velvet quilt, with gentle rises and falls as the boat drifted on its axis. The town, ancient and stoic, stood a glorious orange in the rising light of the sun, its citadel like a sentinel, keeping guard over its magnificent bay. To the left of the town was a harbour and then a sandy beach, and behind it all stood a grandiose mountain range, snow capped and out of focus behind a haunting shroud of fog. The sun hit the back of his neck and he felt exhilarated, he felt alive for the first time in twenty, thirty, forty years. The pain in his spine faded from his consciousness and the stabbing in his gut all but disappeared. He lifted himself to the deck with his wiry, fraught muscles, twisted and sinewy with the trials of life, and he walked to the edge of the boat. He attached his snorkel, and with an elegant dive, his last dive, as good a dive as he'd ever done, he surrendered himself to the sea.

The sea wasn't Africa, Raymond thought, for Africa was populated by people while the sea was not, people who brought power and ego and destruction. Instead the sea was pure. Pure water and pure nature. And yet the sea was Africa, for its truest self was still wild and untamed. Man had tried to kill Africa, just like man tries to kill the sea, but in the long story of the world, the story which had barely even begun, man would lose out, of this Raymond was sure. If Africa was Raymond's soulmate, then the sea was his favourite mistress, and being immersed in it now was as erotic an experience as the tangled legs of seven lovers. As he swam towards the peninsula which hugged the bay, he glided over dazzling schools of tiny fish. Occasionally one would abandon the group to inspect the intruder. He meant them no harm, of course he didn't, his days of causing harm to nature were long over. Come to me little fish, he thought, come and nibble at me and shit me out and make me one with your world. Your world is better than mine. My world is rubbish.

As he glided through the water with impressive ease, Raymond felt young again. When he was just a boy still studying at Edinburgh's famous George Watson's College, he was easily the finest swimmer they'd seen in a generation. As he got older he'd swim whenever he could, for hours on end without bothering to count how many laps. He famously once even swam through crocodile infested waters in the Congo. Now he swam again, and he relished the freedom he felt.

When he arrived at the peninsula he lifted himself from the water and bathed in the sun. His beard, matted together with the salt of the sea, released a steady stream of drips like an unsteady faucet. For an hour or more Raymond remained silent and still, his eyes focused on the horizon, as he watched the sea birds dip and dive for their morning feed. It was remarkable how well he felt, how optimistic everything seemed. He longed for his pipe, which of course he hadn't brought, but otherwise everything was just as it ought to be. He looked towards the yacht, far far away now, and could see no motion, then he looked towards the sun and judged that it was barely eight in the morning. Time to explore, he thought, as he reattached his snorkel and lowered himself amongst the rocks, careful not to tread on the many anemones at home within them. I won't hurt you either, he thought.

He paddled around to the right over a bed of seaweed while several large, silver fish trailed behind him. He looked for anything of extra curiosity, hoping to find an eel or a cuttlefish or perhaps even a seahorse. What if I see a shark, he wondered, are there even sharks in these waters? Will my heart race and propel me the other way, or will I remain still and unafraid? He wanted to think he'd remain still, but if there was a shark lurking around the point that morning he'd never live to see it.

Raymond's life, like his flawed biography, could be easily categorised into two distinct columns. Truth and fiction. The truth column contained adventures and affairs most men could only ever dream of. There were movie star lovers and nights spent sleeping alongside prides of lions. But Raymond couldn't help himself and his inclination towards embellishment had made him a living, breathing joke later in life. It made his fiction column swell to the point where it exploded. He was the boy who cried wolf, except he had actually always seen the wolf. But if it weren't actually a wolf and just a large dog or maybe even a fox what did that matter? And what if it were just a regular domesticated cat? Well who cares, the story is more interesting if it's a wolf, right?

As Raymond took in a breath of air and descended into a cave about a metre below the surface, all of this became shockingly apparent to him. For if he did lie, sometimes, or better yet—embellished, he didn't always. And this would be another of those moments where he'd be unfairly dismissed as a charlatan.

In front of him, in this tiny cave off the coast of Corsica, was an enormous, blindingly bright, lion-fish, looking directly at him. It appeared out of the darkness like an apparition, a ghost. He'd seen one before, years ago off the coast near his own home, and no-one believed him. Scientifically impossible, they'd mutter, dismissing him with a wave of a hand. Lion-fish have never called the Mediterranean home, you old fool. But here he was, staring one down once again, and he'd be damned if he'd be called a fool this time.

The fish didn't move, it just watched him, its red and white frills swaying in the current like flames dancing upon a bonfire.

Raymond lunged. With fingers out-stretched he grabbed the fish and wrestled it towards him. As it fluttered around in his grip it flicked up the sediment beneath them and Raymond lost his vision in the cloud of sand which engulfed him.

Then he felt a sudden pain in his chest, like the violent blow of a spear. He squeezed the fish harder. You bastard, he thought, you've beaten me now, haven't you, and who'll believe any of this when I'm dead. Not wanting to hurt the animal more than he already had, he released it and it darted away. Raymond, suddenly feeling weak, reached up to his left pectoral muscle, and felt around until he found the barb. With steady fingers he gripped its tip and slowly slid it out from inside his wound. It was about seven inches long, and five of those inches had been inside him, the very tip having pierced his heart.

As Raymond let the barb slip away from his weakening grip, the water around him cleared and he saw the fish hovering opposite him, about two metres away. It looked at him for a moment, and then as gently as the night it turned away and vanished out of sight. Well done, Raymond thought, go on victorious fish, go back to your cave, forget about the old man who tried to hurt you. Live a long life, little fish. Live and be strong and enjoy the sea.

As Raymond floated towards the surface, an excruciating pain built up in his chest and he experienced the sensation of his limbs going numb. He only just managed to slip off his goggles as he lifted his head above the surface. He looked towards the boat and could see movement on it now. Everyone would be waking up he figured, wondering where he was, wondering when he'd be back. He went to shout out to them but there was no voice, no breath even.

Think of something intelligent, he urged himself, every man dies thinking of something which no man had ever thought of before him, something which makes everything else make sense. But there was nothing, no in-

telligent thoughts to anchor his life to meaning. And so
instead he tried to remember the name of that damned
song the gardener used to whistle, but he couldn't remember that either. But then he remembered Paul, and
he managed to smile. In a savage last moment of life,
Raymond Bishop's face contorted into something awful
and he descended beneath the sea. It wasn't Africa, but
it was close.

It would do.

No one on the yacht thought to look for Raymond
until after sunset. He is probably just flirting with the
waitresses in the bars, they all agreed. But by then, as
the sun had departed for the day, his body—or what
was left of it, at least—was far out to sea, having been
dragged there by adolescent dolphins, thinking it an
exciting toy.

<h1 style="text-align:center">28</h1>

Paul Greene had become something of a minor celebrity in Tangiers. In the months since having arrived, he'd left the Hotel Continental and moved into an apartment next to the Cinema Rif, a movie theatre which doubled as a bar at the heart of the famed Grand Socco.

He'd begun taking photos again, having found a Rolleiflex Automat camera in an antique store in the casbah, and created a project for himself. Day and night, Paul would traverse the alley ways and squares of the city taking portraits of just about everyone he'd meet. In a single day he could photograph a hundred or more, depending on the willingness of his subjects and the availability of the film. Then, in the evening, he'd set about developing in his makeshift darkroom in the spare room of his apartment. Life had something akin to purpose again.

What he'd do with the photos he wasn't sure, but he made a copy of each portrait to deliver to the subjects should they ever ask for one, and the return to the craft which had made him famous relieved Paul of the nihilism which had brought him to Tangiers in the first place. He never paused to think of Vanessa or Rebecca, Samia or Raymond, for they represented a life he'd left behind, a life best forgotten. Rather he immersed himself in the local community, where he had numerous acquaintances but no true friends, just how he liked it, and they in turn accepted the tall and handsome Australian as one of their own.

One afternoon, as the sun blanketed the sky with pink and orange hues, hues which reminded him of France, Paul sat at the bar at the Cinema Rif and finished off a beer.

"Excuse me," a voice behind him interrupted his thoughts, "you are the photographer, Paul Greene, are you not?"

Paul turned around on his stool to find a young woman behind him, she was thin and wiry with large black spectacles and a miserable little streak of lipstick hiding her mouth. Paul had seen her many times before, sitting in the corner of the bar with her nose always deep in a textbook. Her English was heavily accented and she had the uneasy confidence of an adolescent intellectual.

"I am," Paul replied, swirling his beer in his glass as he hunched over the bar, "and you are?"

"My name is Farida, do you mind if I sit with you?"

"Why not," Paul shrugged, "there's nothing else going on today."

Farida dumped her books on the bar next to Paul and climbed onto a stool. Then she placed an odd looking box with a microphone attached on the stool next to her.

"So, how'd you know my name?" Paul asked.

"I'm sorry," Farida conceded, "I should have been

more up-front. I am a student here, at the cinema, and I am studying to be a cinematographer. My professor, a very wise man who once worked with Burtolucci, encourages us students to study photographers, not just other cinematographers. One day, reading the archives in his study, I came across a book of your pictures. I straight away thought they were very powerful."

"That's nice of you to say so," Paul lamented, "it's been a long time since I've heard anyone talk about my work."

"Well I could hardly believe it when I recognised you sitting at this bar. It's taken me weeks to work up the courage to speak to you."

"You shouldn't be afraid like that, that's not the way to live life. So, what is it you're after? A portrait, an autograph, advice?"

"No, none of that, an interview. What I would like is an interview."

"What about?"

"Your photos, of course. Your technique, your method, your philosophy."

"And if I told you I have no technique, no method, no philosophy?"

"I wouldn't believe you," she said, completely stone faced. "I've seen your work, there is definitely some rhyme and reason to it, although at the same time perhaps it is anarchistic. So perhaps you are not lying, that's what I'd like to find out."

Paul sat silent for a moment and considered his options. The girl seemed genuine, intelligent too, and he was doubtful she had any shady motives. But his career was still something of a sore spot for him, it took him back to Sydney, which took him back to Vanessa. Still, he had fallen in love with it again over the recent weeks, and if he could help Farida out then he may atone for some of his sins. There were a lot of sins.

"What's it for?" he asked. "Who's going to read it?"

"For my class," she shrugged, "and my own archives. I hope to have an archive like my professor one day. Maybe too it could go online, I have a friend who owns an online magazine about the Moroccan art scene."

"No," Paul shook his head, "it can't go online."

"Ok," Farida conceded, noticing the sudden shift in Paul's energy, "it doesn't have to go online."

Paul readjusted himself on his stool and looked at the young woman. "Where would you like to do it then?" he asked. "My apartment is just next door, I could show you my own darkroom and all the equipment I have collected in Tangiers."

"It's ok, let's just do it here," she suggested, "I love the hum of the Cinema Rif, it will make for a nice soundtrack. Unless you are busy this afternoon? Then we could arrange to do it tomorrow."

"Me? Busy?" Paul laughed. "I haven't been busy my whole life. Sure, let's do it here."

Farida reached for the box with the microphone and placed it in front of them. She propped herself up taller on her stool, to come closer to Paul's height, and flicked through a notebook where she'd already prepared some questions. She pressed the record button and cleared her throat while Paul gestured to the bartender for another beer. When it arrived he took a sip and cleared his own throat, then he spun around to face her and was surprised to find himself suddenly nervous.

"When you're ready," he encouraged her.

Farida moved the microphone to her own mouth, and began an introduction. "I'm sitting here with Paul Greene, photographer extraordinaire, at the bar of the Cinema Rif in Tangiers. Paul's career spans many decades, and has included stints as a private photographer for the former president of the U.S., Ronald Reagan, countless covers for magazines such as Vogue and Vanity Fair, and hard-hitting photojournalism essays throughout the developing world, including here in Africa. Paul, let me start by asking you, why Tangiers?"

"Why not?" Paul shrugged. "A man has to be somewhere, right?"

Farida laughed, and for the first time since their meeting she seemed to relax a little. "Sure," she said, "a man must be somewhere. But don't you agree there are other places that a world famous photographer might want to pass his days?"

"No," Paul disagreed, "Tangiers has always attracted artists. Since its days as an international zone it has been the ideal place for a man to disappear in, to hideaway without being found."

"And what are you hiding from?" she asked.

"The past, I suppose," he said, sipping his beer.

"Could it be argued that you're also hiding from the future?"

The girl was smart, Paul thought, and he was surprised to find he was enjoying the interview.

"A man of my years doesn't need a future, the future belongs to you, not me."

"Then what do you wake up for everyday? What motivates you?"

"It's a struggle, I'll admit. Some mornings I wake up

and lay there staring at the ceiling fan for what must be hours. I'll get up and shower and throw on whatever clothes are strewn across the floor and then I'll climb back into bed and wish the day would just finish already. But I've started photographing again lately, just portraits of local people, that gives me some hope."

"And before you started that project?"

"Nothing," he conceded, "there was nothing for me."

Farida and Paul both remained silent. Out of nowhere she pressed stop on the recorder and looked at Paul, she thought she could see a tear.

"Mr. Greene, if you'd prefer we could do this another time," she suggested.

Paul shook his head, "It's fine, we can continue."

Farida reached over and pressed the button with the big red circle. The bar was getting crowded now, and she held the microphone a little closer to her mouth to be heard more clearly.

"When did you know you wanted to be a photographer?"

"It's a sad story, actually."

"You don't have to answer then, if you'd prefer not to."

"No, it's really fine. I was young, about nineteen, and I was on a path to nowhere. One evening I'd broken into a house that belonged to an elderly German man in my neighbourhood. He'd once called the police on me for lingering in the park next to his house, and the police gave me a good beating. Naturally I wanted to get some revenge on the old bastard. I waited until it was an especially dark night and I broke into his house through a side window. Inside his house I snuck around as quietly as I could but all I could find worth taking were a small bag of old coins, an antique pistol and a camera. I took the whole lot. I managed to sell the coins and the pistol for a small amount of money but no-one wanted the camera. I noticed it was engraved with a small love letter on its base and I suddenly felt terrible. I mean, maybe it was a memento from the war or something. And so I went to return it, and as I approached his house, to leave the damn thing hanging on his fence, there was an ambulance out the front. The man had had a heart-attack and died soon after. So I kept the camera. I had a friend teach me how to use it, and I've never stopped taking pictures."

"Do you still have it?" she asked.

"No," Paul shook his head, "it was destroyed in a house fire a few months ago."

Farida readjusted herself to change the tone of the interview. Paul ordered another drink.

"For a short time you were the photographer for Ronald Reagan, how was that?"

"The parties were fun," he laughed.

"And what about your work with models?"

"Fun too, I mean, I did marry one after all."

"A large part of your career was spent here in Africa, do you feel a connection to this continent?"

Paul nodded and took a drink. "Very much so, I've always said Africa had the finest people in the world and I stand by that today."

Farida smiled, "That's very sweet of you to say, Mr. Greene."

"Well, it's the truth. Although Africa is very different today than how I remember it years ago."

"That brings me to a former colleague of yours, Raymond Bishop. He never reached the heights of fame that you did, but it seems you two were an inseparable pair at certain points of your careers. Especially that exposé you did together in the Congo, documenting the struggle of the local tribes against the miners."

"Raymond Bishop…" Paul started before trailing off, "Raymond Bishop is a complicated and complicating man. His good attributes outweigh his bad, but his bad is where he likes to live his life."

"*Was*," Farida corrected him.

"Sorry?" Paul asked.

"You said Raymond *is* a complicated man, I'm just correcting you, ignore me, sorry."

"I don't follow," Paul said, shifting uneasily on his barstool.

"You don't believe he's dead then? You believe the theory that he's just hiding out somewhere on the island?"

"Wait a minute," Paul demanded, "please, stop recording."

Farida reached over and pressed stop on her machine.

"You don't know then," she whispered, almost to herself.

"I don't know what?"

"Raymond Bishop is dead, Mr. Greene, he went missing off the coast of Corsica two months ago. It was all over the news, I thought for sure you would have known."

Paul reached into his pocket and pulled out a few loose notes and handed them to the bartender. "Is there an internet cafe nearby?" he asked Farida with a desperate intensity.

"Yes," she said, surprised to find her voice shaking,

"just off the Grand Socco, down that street there," she directed him, pointing.

"Good luck with your course, you'll do fine," Paul said, as he charged out of the Cinema Rif.

29

Paul hadn't slept well in days. From Tangiers he'd flown back to Marseille, and from Marseille he'd taken the train to Toulon. From Toulon he'd ridden the bus for three hours until he reached the village. He needed to find out from Denise, from Achille, from Samia, from anyone—what exactly had happened to Raymond.

As he entered the cafe he was disturbed to discover he recognised no-one, none of the staff nor the clientele were familiar to him. Had the town changed so much in such a short time? he wondered. He took a seat at the counter and waited for the attention of the young woman behind the bar. She was a large woman, and in the narrow confines of her workspace she moved with the awkwardness of a large beast in a too small cage.

"Excuse me," Paul said in his clumsy French.

"I'll be with you in a moment," the woman replied, dismissively.

As he sat there Paul considered his options. Everything he'd read online had suggested that Raymond was dead, however without the proof of a corpse there would always be the small chance that he'd somehow survived. Paul had considered taking the ferry to Corsica and spending a month or two asking around the island, snooping around like an amateur detective and seeing what he could discover. But first he needed to speak to someone here. Eventually the woman finished chatting with the other customers and made her way over to him.

"What would you like?" she asked as she leaned over the bar, utterly uninterested in the transaction.

"I'm looking for someone," Paul said, "she owns this bar, or used to, at least."

"You mean Denise?" she responded, dryly.

"Yes, Denise, exactly. Is she in today?"

"She sold the place, she doesn't work here anymore."

"Impossible," Paul scoffed, "this cafe was her life."

"Not anymore, her life is all glitz and glamour these days."

"I don't follow."

"Her boyfriend, the fool of a farmer who lived by the sea, he won big in Saint-Tropez, and now they live there."

"You mean Achille?"

"How would I know his name?" the woman retorted. "Talk to my uncle over there, he's the one who bought it from her."

The barkeep gestured to a man in the corner sitting in front of a laptop. He wore a pinstripe suit and his hair was slicked back like a gangster.

"Sorry to interrupt," Paul approached the man. "But I'm looking for some friends, and you may be able to help."

The man explained to Paul that Achille had made a small fortune on roulette in the casino in Saint-Tropez. At first Denise had been furious to find out he'd gambled away the money he'd made from the sale of Paul's property for the second time, but when Achille transferred all the winnings into her account, they had a shotgun wedding and purchased a small apartment overlooking the bay. The cafe owner gave Paul Denise's number, and Paul took a cab to the small city to try and find her.

Paul hadn't visited Saint-Tropez before, despite it being the biggest draw in the region by a long shot. As he approached the town he looked out the window at the tranquil water, reflecting the sky as the morning woke up slowly, and he felt a lazy peacefulness in the air. He paid the cabdriver and walked around until he found a payphone. The town itself was charming, with elegant apartment buildings pressed together closely amongst small whitewashed restaurants and taverns. Along the promenade that flanked the harbour he admired the sailing boats and super yachts, all of them branded with the flags of far-flung tax havens like Bermuda or the Cayman Islands. He thought of Raymond.

Eventually Paul found a pay-phone and he called Denise. It only rang once before she answered.

"*Bonjour*," she said.

"Denise, it's Paul," he responded, finding it difficult to hear her over the crackling phone. "I need to talk about Raymond."

There was silence on the other end, as Paul glanced around at the sea behind him while the wind whipped at his hair.

"Paul," she said eventually, "where are you?"

"I'm in Saint-Tropez, at a pay-phone by the wharf, I need to see you. Urgently."

"Look up," she said after a moment, her smile clear in her voice. "To your right."

Paul glanced out of the box and looked to where she'd instructed him. On a third floor balcony, still wearing her pyjamas, Paul could see Denise waving enthusiastically.

"Wait there," she said, "I'll be with you in a moment."

When Denise eventually joined Paul on the waterfront, he was surprised at just how youthful she looked. The dark bags that had hung under her eyes, the battle scars of sixteen hour shifts, day after day, had all but disappeared. Her hair, permanently greying at the roots with miserable orange tips, was now a brilliant blonde that framed her face like an artwork. She was wearing makeup, something he'd never noticed her do before, and she wore a vibrant blue summer dress which gave her the air of a young honeymooner. The change was dramatic and he couldn't help but wonder how Achille must look.

"Come," she said, linking her arm with his, "let's share a bottle of rosé and we can tell each other everything. Confess to all our dirty secrets."

"Let's," Paul agreed, as she led him away from the water.

They found a spot on the balcony of a nautical bar which overlooked the harbour and the tiny mountains opposite, and they ordered a bottle of Italian wine and sank into their chairs as the sunlight streaked across them.

"It's beautiful here," Paul said.

"It is," Denise agreed, "but only if you have money, otherwise it may as well be a slum."

"You sold the cafe?" Paul asked.

"I did," Denise nodded, "I was hesitant at first, worried I'd be too bored without it. But I am an old woman now and I've earnt my rest."

"You're not nearly as old as I am Denise, and I'm as restless as I've ever been. I don't know if I'll ever settle in one spot again."

"Well, I have some news Paul, which may make that easier for you," she said as she sipped her wine.

"Go on," Paul instructed.

Denise reached into her designer purse and pulled out a white envelope. She opened it and unfolded a photocopied piece of paper.

"Here," she said, handing it to him.

Paul couldn't believe what he was looking at. It was Raymond's will, dated the week before he'd vanished, and he'd left his house and all his belongings to Paul and Samia. A fifty-fifty split.

"Well?" Denise prodded him.

"I don't know what to say. I mean, I don't need the money, I'm perfectly fine. He should have left it all to the girl."

"It's not too late," Denise shrugged. "You could always transfer your half to her."

"Yes, I must," he agreed. "How do I contact her?"

Denise shook her head. Paul felt his pulse start racing.

"What's wrong?" he asked.

"Nothing. It's just…" she trailed off.

"What?"

"No-one knows where she is Paul, after what happened with Raymond, she disappeared too. I've tried to track her down, I've had people visit her family in Paris and they won't admit to knowing anything. I spoke to that Greek girl and her father and all they could tell me is she disappeared a couple of months into the search for Raymond in Corsica."

'I have to find her," Paul said.

"No," Denise put her hand on him. "When she wants to be found she'll show up."

"What if something has happened to her?"

"Well if something's happened to her then it's happened, what can you possibly do to fix anything? You need to finish reading the will, there's a stipulation."

Paul looked back at the paper, and was shocked by what he saw. In order for the will to be activated, it required Paul to return to the house and with the help of decades of letters and diaries and correspondence, to write a new biography of Raymond. An honest one, without all the bullshit.

"But I'm not a writer," Paul said.

"Well you'd better learn," Denise smiled. "Otherwise the poor girl will get none of it. Do it for her, Paul."

Paul nodded and returned his attention to the view.

After a while he spoke again. "Do you think he's dead, Denise? Do you think he's really dead this time or just hiding out in some dimly lit bar in a no-where town chatting up the local peasant girls?"

"He's dead," Denise said, as matter of factly as anything she'd ever said in her life.

"But how do you know?" Paul asked.

"I'm a woman, we have a way of knowing if a man is dead or merely dying. And Raymond is dead."

"How about me?" Paul asked. "Am I dead or dying?"

"You've been dying ever since you lost your wife. Your daughter's murder sped it up a little, but there's still some life in you left. And what is left you must harness for the sake of Samia. Now, finish your wine and follow me, I want you to see Achille, you'll hardly believe how he dresses these days."

30

It wasn't hard to find a publisher for Raymond's biography. It'd taken Paul months to go through the mountains of papers and letters Raymond had collected throughout his life, which he'd left in a huge pile in his study the day before he'd taken the boat to Corsica. There were school reports from his childhood, Christmas cards he'd made for his parents that he'd kept for more than seventy years. There were diaries from his early days working for small town newspapers throughout Scotland and later England. There were letters from lovers, never before seen photographs from war-zones, divorce settlements and vitriolic back-and-forths with critics. There was even a list of phone numbers, more than a few hundred in total, which Paul could call if he needed any more information, and Paul was depressed to find more than half were already dead, most having died long ago. He'd kept every article he'd ever written, as well as a diary for every year of his adult life. Paul felt he owed it to his friend to tell his story as honestly as possible, and so he read every piece with astute attention.

When it came to the actual writing, Paul enlisted the help of a former colleague of theirs who'd retired from the BBC a few years earlier, and he acted as a ghost-writer when there was a sequence Paul couldn't quite solve. While he took a lot of joy from revisiting Raymond's life, he'd also suffered a lot of pain. One photo in particular, of a very young Raymond, his eyes wild and alive, his smile devilishly handsome, with his arm around a tired looking Albert Camus hit Paul particularly hard. Paul had always accused Raymond of being a fraud, and in his later years Raymond had resigned himself to copping the barbs rather than fending them off. By the time the book was ready to be launched it'd taken over a year and a half.

Paul had sworn to never visit Paris again, but the publisher insisted it was the perfect city to launch the book in. Hadn't Raymond lived in Paris, after all, when he was a young and struggling writer who'd barely survived off scraps of bread old women had thrown to the pigeons. Was it not apt that the city in which he'd struggled so terribly be the city in which he was to be redeemed? Initially Paul resisted and battled to have the book launched in Edinburgh instead, it was after all his home town. But it was a phone call Paul received one afternoon, sitting in the study in Raymond's house in Gassin, that changed everything.

"Hello?" Paul answered in English, as almost everyone who called him these days was a native English speaker helping with the biography.

"Hello," the voice whispered down the line, "is that you, Paul?"

"It is," he replied.

"Ok, good."

"Samia?" Paul asked, stunned.

The line went silent.

"Samia?" he repeated.

"Yes, Paul, it is me."

"Where are you? I'd almost given up."

"I'm back in Paris."

As soon as they'd finished their conversation Paul rang his publisher and much to their surprise he agreed with them enthusiastically. "Yes, it must be launched in Paris, you are right, of course, no other city will do, Paris is the city that defines him. Let's do it next month. No, sooner, let's just do it as quickly as possible!"

Now, weeks after that phone call, he sat on the street at a cafe in Montparnasse and ordered his second coffee as he waited for Samia to arrive. He was nervous, his feet tapping beneath the table and his hands fumbling with a loose cigarette he'd found in his brown overcoat. He was surrounded by Parisians, real Parisians, reading the morning edition of La Monde while sipping espressos and offering indifferent glances at the commotion on the street. He'd always loved the French way of enjoying coffee, seated facing the sidewalk while watching the parade of passerbys go about their day. He looked at his phone, it was 12:15, she was late. He thought about paying his bill and leaving, what was he even going to say to her? Would she forgive him, he wondered, for the way he'd spoken to her at their last meeting? He was brash and rude and dismissive, why on earth would she want to see him again? He was downright horrible.

Then he saw her, appearing from the crowd like an

apparition on a moonless night. She wore a red coat, a black beret and red lipstick. Her skin was paler than he'd remembered it, and her hair, electric black, was pulled back with a single strand dangling luxuriously over her brow. She approached him and he stood up, awkwardly bumping the small, round table and causing his coffee to spill a little. He nervously put out his hand to shake hers, but she ignored it and instead kissed him on the right cheek, and then the left.

"We don't shake hands in Paris, Paul," she smiled.

"I know," he said shaking his head, "I've been doing everything wrong all day."

"Just all day?" she laughed.

"Fair call," he smiled.

"Shall we sit?" she asked.

"Of course," he replied, as they each took a seat.

For a moment they said nothing and just smiled at one another. He looked older, she thought, but still handsome, somehow, while he couldn't believe how youthful she seemed.

"I..." he started, and then trailed off.

"Yes?" she asked.

"I wanted to say sorry."

"Don't Paul, what's done is done."

"But I was horrible."

"Please, Paul, be quiet. We are different now, everything is different."

"You're right, of course."

"And what about Paris? Is Paris different for you? You once told me you'd never return and yet—here you are."

"It is, definitely," he agreed. "Last time I was here it was cold, calculating. Now it seems fresh again, like the morning after a storm."

Samia said nothing and looked away. A waiter came over and she ordered a glass of wine.

"You don't mind, do you?" she asked him.

"Of course not, do as you like."

"I promise I won't keep drinking, you won't have to worry about me being too drunk tonight. Embarrassing you in front of all the important people."

"So you will be there, then?"

"Yes, I couldn't miss it, not for anything. Will you do a speech?"

"I have to, right?"

"I suppose so. Have you written one?"

"Just the intro."

"How does it go?"

He reached into his trouser pocket and retrieved a piece of paper. He unfolded it and cleared his throat. Then he read.

"Raymond Bishop was a difficult man, I should know—he's the only person who's ever shot me, blown up my house and tried to steal my wife."

Samia laughed.

"Save it," she said. "I want to hear the rest tonight."

He folded it and put it away as the waiter brought over her wine. She took a sip.

"I miss him Paul," she said, lowering the glass.

"Me too," Paul admitted.

"It was so terrible when we lost him."

"I can't imagine."

"No, you can't. The night before he was reflective, he was gentle. He told me about his parents, did you know his father was killed here in France, during the war?

That's why he'd chosen to live here, to be close to his father's memory. Just like you with Vanessa. Of course you know that, you've written a book about him. But before he went to sleep that night he told me he loved me, not in a romantic way but in a daughterly way, and he kissed me on the hair as he cradled my chin. The next day I didn't even bother to look for him until after sunset, I figured he'd just gone for a swim and a walk somewhere. Then when it was dark I became scared, inconsolable. We looked everywhere in town, it's not a big town and he was no where. I stayed on the island for two months, going north to south and east to west, showing everyone the photograph of him and I, the one you took in front of the fountain at his house. Katerina and her father eventually had enough of me. They left me with a sum of money and I never spoke to either of them again. After a while my own father had to fly down to rescue me and bring me back to Paris. I went mad, Paul."

"I'm so sorry," Paul said.

"You should be," she reprimanded him, tears welling up in her eyes. "Because the only thing that could have helped all that time was being with you. Together we could have found him, I know it."

"He's dead, Samia," he said.

"You don't know that."

"I do," he said. "I just know."

"Well what if he is," Samia said, now crying. "We can still search of him, can't we?"

"We don't have to, Samia, I found him, writing the book I found Raymond."

"And what about Vanessa?" she asked.

"What about Vanessa?"

"Have you found her, Paul?"

Paul shook his head.

"Why not?"

"I don't know where to look."

"Look here," she said, wiping her tears away and staring at him. "Look right here," she repeated as she leant in and kissed him. He kissed her back.

"Where did you disappear to?" she asked, pulling away and resting her hand in his.

"Tangiers," he replied.

She laughed.

"What's funny?" he asked.

"You don't see the irony?"

Paul shook his head.

"Don't worry then. But why the hell did you go to Tangiers?"

"I don't know," he admitted, "isn't that what broken people do? Disappear in Tangiers?"

"If you say so. Are you going to go back?"

"Maybe, I don't know. Once the book is released tonight the house is yours, Raymond's house, you can do with it as you please."

"I'll sell it," she said, "my parents could use the money more than I could use a house."

"That's very generous."

"But you have money, don't you Paul?"

"I do, plenty."

"Then we're going to be fine together, aren't we?"

"We are," Paul nodded.

Suddenly Samia turned and gestured to the waiter for the bill. He brought it over, Paul paid and they left the cafe.

"Well, what now?" he asked.

"I want to take you somewhere," Samia said, reaching for his hand.

"Where?"

"I want to show you where Vanessa was killed," she replied as she lead him along the boulevard.

"I don't know if I'm ready," he said, pulling away.

"It's not about you Paul, it's about her, she'd like to see us like this."

"I don't know, Samia, really."

"Please, Paul," she said, stopping on the sidewalk. "I've waited so long for you to come and find me again, so, so long while you were in stupid Tangiers doing nothing. Please don't disappoint me any more than you already have," she pleaded.

"Ok, you're right, of course. Let's go see Vanessa."

"*Merci*," she said, and then she kissed him once more.

They began walking again, hand in hand, and vanished into the sombre Parisian crowd. The man was completely broken and the woman was utterly lost, but at least now they knew for sure—the other could never be alone again.

www.ingramcontent.com/pod-product-compliance
Lightning Source LLC
Chambersburg PA
CBHW020129120726
47903CB00007B/2174